PENGUIN BEACH

With Love

PENGUIN BEACH

A NEW ARRIVAL

Lawrence Prestidge

Matador
9 Priory Business Park,
Wistow Road, Kibworth Beauchamp,
Leicestershire. LE8 0RX
Tel: 0116 279 2299
Email: books@troubador.co.uk
Web: www.troubador.co.uk/matador
Twitter: @matadorbooks

ISBN 978 1838594 862

British Library Cataloguing in Publication Data.
A catalogue record for this book is available from the British Library.

Printed and bound by CPI Group (UK) Ltd, Croydon, CR0 4YY
Typeset in 12pt Book Antiqua by Troubador Publishing Ltd, Leicester, UK

Matador is an imprint of Troubador Publishing Ltd

Dedicated to the amazing
workers of the NHS

'Not all heroes wear capes'

STARRING:

DIEGO

CLYDE

NAHYA

PRESTON & PIERCE

YOHANN
ARTHUR
ANTON
RAY
BOBBY & PAM

ONE

"Encore! Encore!" the crowd at London Zoo cheered as Clyde graciously took his final bow. He had been a resident at London Zoo for many years after being transferred from a zoo in Dublin, Ireland. Life in the zoo was all he knew and he loved it. While visitors came from near and far to visit the famous Penguin Beach, Clyde was the big star and everybody knew it. Well known for performing his Irish dancing, Clyde delighted in performing for the growing crowds, receiving their applause long after he flopped down from his 'stage' and joined his fellow comrades for dinner.

"Look lively everyone! Dinner is here!" called Arthur as Clyde rejoined the group. A tall King Penguin and no doubt the wisest in the

group, Arthur jumped up from where he'd been sleeping and was already halfway towards the keeper before Clyde had even registered the tall waterproofed figure entering their enclosure.

"I guess it's boring old fish again," Ray, a gentoo penguin, moaned. Clyde rolled his eyes but luckily only Arthur caught him – giving him a stern shake of the head before turning back towards the keeper eagerly. To Clyde, it seemed that Ray did very little but moan; moaning about food, moaning about the weather. Boy, could Ray moan about anything! In particular, though, Ray moaned about the cold. He hated being cold. Imagine that? A penguin who objected to the temperature.

The rest of the flock caught up and bustled around the keeper, and as Clyde looked back round, he wasn't surprised to see that not everyone was getting involved. Standing in the shadows of their cave, making every effort not to be noticed, was Yohann. A 'rockhopper penguin' from France, Yohann didn't seem to trust anyone or, in fact, like anyone very much. He certainly kept himself to himself and could often be found in the corner of Penguin Beach looking at the other penguins with dagger-like stares. Keeping his cards close to his chest, no one knew much of what Yohann was thinking – that is until visiting time began.

"Why must you use a phone?! LOOK! Open your eyes!" He would often vent, expressing his hatred of the phones and devices that were thrust into the penguins' faces day in day out.

He found it even more frustrating seeing visitors rely on their phones for other parts of their lives.

"Where should we go to eat after, dear?" he would hear one gentleman say to his wife.

"I'm not sure, honey, let me see what I can find on Google," his wife would reply as she pulled her phone out to check.

Seeing this made Yohann's blood boil!

"You're in London! Why don't you walk around and look, you idiots? Why must you ask your phone?! Are you stupid?! LIVE YOUR LIFE!" He would often scream - though of course, to the visitors of the zoo, this translated as a delightful display of penguin enthusiasm, prompting yet more camera phones and videoing.

As Clyde reached up to the keeper to catch an outstretched fish in his beak, he was knocked aside in a whirlwind of black and white. Pierce and Preston had arrived. Bounding confidently towards the keeper, Pierce and Preston showed no regard for their fellow penguins when it came to mealtimes. As two erect-crested penguins who had been in London for a couple of years, Pierce and Preston came from a zoo in Las Vegas – a fact that more than explained their flashy attitudes and confidence which bordered on arrogance. They would often pass their time looking out of Penguin Beach at the human visitors and critiquing their outfits.

"Goodness, Pierce, look at her dress – did a grape attack her?" Preston would mutter.

"At least the accessories are a saving grace," Pierce would reply back.

No sooner had the terrible twosome moved aside, than Clyde heard another squeal. "Yipee! Gary, look! Dinner!" – it was Anton, the chinstrap penguin. Though addressed as if he were one of the gang, Gary was in fact a soft toy penguin which Anton had found after a child left it near Penguin Beach. He had kept it ever since – he was under the assumption, however, that it was a real penguin who just happened to be extremely shy, and no one quite had the heart to put him right. Anton certainly wasn't the smartest of penguins. In fact, he was about as sharp as a bowling ball. With that being said, he was so much fun. He never had any worries or troubles and was just an energetic little penguin that lived in the moment.

"Perhaps we could all learn a lesson from Anton," Pierce had once said to Preston.

"Learn a lesson from Anton? I once saw him pee in his own face and smile!" Preston replied distastefully.

As Clyde stood plotting his route back into the frenzy that dinner time had, yet again, become, suddenly there was Nayha. Clyde sighed as he looked over at her gracefully heading towards the carnage. Nayha, like Clyde, was a Magellanic penguin and though the two of them got on very well, Clyde couldn't help but feel shy around her. Most evenings, once dinner time was over and the group had dispersed, they would look at the night time sky together and soak in the moon and the stars.

Momentarily lost in the memory of the previous evening's stargazing, Clyde's mind was abruptly snapped back to reality as he realised Nayha was coming towards him. "Come on silly! Aren't you coming for dinner? The keeper's here – you must have worked up quite the appetite after another brilliant performance." With her final comment Nayha dropped her majestic head in a mock bow, causing Clyde to grin as he happily came to join her.

As they approached the group and the smell of fish awoke Clyde's stomach with a rumbling start, Nayha paused and turned to him. "It's great having someone bring us fish every day but do you ever wonder what it would be like out of the zoo? Just being free?" she asked.

"Sometimes," Clyde replied carefully. "But I'm happy. Because if it wasn't for the zoo, I wouldn't be here with you - and we wouldn't be able to make all those people happy every day," he added.

The truth was, Clyde did often ponder what the world was like outside the zoo, and sometimes found that hours had passed with him just imagining a world outside their glistening blue water, glass panels and careful rock formations. But one thing was for certain, Clyde loved his home. After all, he was the big star of Penguin Beach. He loved dancing and entertaining the crowds of people, and he absolutely loved the cheering and applause he got. All the other penguins looked up to him. In truth, they needed Clyde to keep the audiences entertained and to keep the crowds coming, and it didn't take a genius to see why.

They were an eclectic group, certainly, but the others just didn't possess the raw talent reserved only for Clyde. Ray, the moaner, was usually snuggled up in the cave trying to keep warm. Anton (and his stuffed friend Gary) would spend every morning scouting the pool for stray treats, followed by an afternoon of what Anton called 'splishing'. An annoying and highly repetitive habit, 'splishing' involved continually jumping into the pool and hopping back out, over and over again. At first Clyde had thought it was cute and looked forward to seeing an audience gather around Anton, but the routine quickly became repetitive and the visitors had slowly stopped coming. Yohann was usually eyeballing the others in disgust, often doing his best to avoid a stern word from Arthur who – when he wasn't asleep – would spend his days monitoring the performance of the other penguins and offering them detailed reviews of their behaviour. Of course, this was usually interrupted by Pierce and Preston who could often be heard loudly debating the visitors' outfits, and as for Nayha, she was Clyde's cheerleader and his best friend. Seeing Nayha at the side of his stage always inspired a fuzzy feeling in Clyde's chest, and he was sure his best performances were when she was there. Often, he wanted her to join him and would always try to involve her when he could, but these shared performances were rare.

Today Clyde looked around at the small crowd of penguins as they each enjoyed their food. As the keeper threw the fish in the air they would jump and dive for it. All except

Yohann, of course. They were an odd bunch but they were family to him. Then suddenly, just as Nayha elegantly caught the last fish in her beak and Clyde offered her her own round of applause, something unexpected happened.

The gate opened, and in walked another keeper.

"Seconds?!" Pierce shrieked excitedly, dashing forward as fast as his legs would allow.

But the second keeper hadn't come in to serve more food at all. He walked over to the front of their cave and placed a cage down on the floor. As he opened it up and reached in, Clyde heard a murmur of activity around him from his fellow comrades. What was going on?

The keeper's arms slowly retracted from the cage and revealed a penguin the others had never seen before, that looked like he was fast asleep. Then, as quickly as they had arrived, both keepers left Penguin Beach.

Bobby and Pam rolled out of their nest. They were the resident couple of Penguin Beach. Both were snares penguins and had been together for around eight years. They didn't always talk to each other in the most loving way – in fact they rarely talked at all. But every so often you would see that there really was a powerful love between them.

"A new arrival?" Bobby muttered as he sidled up to the others, giving the unfamiliar penguin a wide berth.

"Bobby – shut up!" Pam shouted as she slapped him across the head. "So, do you think it's a newbie?" she politely asked Arthur.

"It seems that way," Arthur answered as he gazed warily at the sleeping penguin. "He's a macaroni penguin – I'm sure of that!" Arthur added.

"You should be careful. I don't trust him," piped Yohann in warning, as he raised his beak up at the new penguin.

"Come on guys, let's be friendly!" Pierce called out.

"Yeah – we should," added Preston backing his friend up. "Me and Pierce love meeting new people. We keep in touch with all our pen pals all the time! Like Casper in the Antarctic, for example, he's always been really friendly with us. Although judging by his latest photos we suspect he may have become a cannibal."

"It's so cold out here…" Ray moaned, backing away towards his cave.

"Gary says we should keep him!" Anton added as he held onto his soft toy and struggled to make his voice heard above the rising chatter of the penguins.

Clyde had heard enough.

"Guys... Guys. Calm down!" Clyde called as he stepped forward. The chatter ceased gradually, just in time for Clyde to catch Ray mutter "Here he goes," under his breath. He chose to ignore that particular comment, and instead continued.

"There's nothing to worry about! This is a good thing! I'll go over there and welcome him okay? He must be nervous! Remember what it was like for some of you when you were new here?"

"Go on then!" Bobby nodded.

"I'm going!" Clyde said as he gingerly walked his way over to the sleeping penguin.

"Helllloooooo!" Clyde muttered as he prodded the penguin with his flipper. "Hey there!" he added – but there was no response.

Spurred on by his comrades and a swift nod from Arthur, Clyde took a big step forward so he was standing right over the new penguin, and leant in close to him to see if there was any sign of life. Clyde took in the neatly styled mohawk – the likes of which he had never seen on a penguin before, and was just about to prod him again when the sleeping penguin's eyes opened suddenly and grew huge. Before he knew it, Clyde was on his back and was pinned down under the new penguin.

"Ahhhhhhh!!!" Preston screamed in an unnaturally high pitch tone. "He's a cannibal!"

He yelled, dashing backwards and forwards and causing a riot of panic amongst the group; who immediately began bashing into each other in a bid to move to help Clyde.

"Who are you? What are you doing?" the penguin asked Clyde through a strong Spanish accent.

"It's okay, it's okay! I'm Clyde – I'm a friend! I was just coming over to check you were okay

– and welcome you. You're in London Zoo. This is Penguin Beach… look… see?" Clyde explained breathlessly, as he struggled to pull himself upright and point towards the other penguins.

The penguin looked hard at Clyde and flicked his eyes towards the rest of the penguins, finally moving aside and letting Clyde go.

"Sorry, amigo – I'm sure you can understand I've been through quite an ordeal," the penguin explained as he offered Clyde a hand.

"Ordeal?" Clyde questioned.

"Yes señor – it's nice to meet another at last. Allow me to introduce myself – I am Diego," he stated with a deep extravagant bow.

"Errrrr… Clyde," replied Clyde stiffly.

"An honour it is, señor Clyde. I must ask you, what is this place? Who are these? Are they amigos or NO amigos?" Diego asked as he glared at the others.

"Oh yeah sure – they're friends, yes – sorry, amigos, I mean. Let me introduce you." He said before calling over the others. "Guys, can you come over here? It's okay!" Clyde added as the rest of the penguins cautiously approached both Clyde and Diego, led by Arthur who strode forward purposely.

"Everybody, this is Diego!" Clyde announced. "Diego, this is… well, everybody."

"Hola!" Diego said as he bowed to the group.

"I already hate him," Yohann grunted, adding, "your accent is ridiculous," in his own very French accent.

"And you are?" Diego asked.

"Why? What does it matter?" Yohann answered again in a very unfriendly manner.

"I can actually speak some French," Diego said conversationally, taking a small step towards Yohann.

"I speak English – don't try!" Yohann replied with a firm shake of the head; crossing his arms for good measure.

"Why, aren't you a handsome bird!" Pam flirted, prompting a disappointed glare from Bobby.

"You are very beautiful yourself, señorita," Diego replied, to make Pam blush.

"Oh, you should have seen me back in my heyday!" she replied before getting out an old photo of her and Bobby to show him.

"That was back when me and Bobby first met at the final of the world ice hockey championships in Iceland! It was an amazing game. Awww look at me there 'ey?"

"You looked very pretty, señorita. What happened?" Diego asked.

"WOAH!" Bobby stepped in, shocked, pushing Pam away from their new comrade.

"Well Diego, I'll have you know that everyone gets older. And just because Pam doesn't look as young as she used to, it doesn't mean…"

"I meant what happened at the ice hockey championships?" Diego interrupted with an amused look on his face.

"Oh." Bobby replied, rather embarrassed, as he received a disapproving glare from Pam.

"Cool hair!" Anton commented as he nodded towards Diego's mohawk, though Clyde noticed that he still kept Gary well hidden from sight behind his back.

"Gracias, amigo!" replied Diego gracefully.

"So, tell us. How did you get here? Where are you from?" questioned Arthur, observing and circling around Diego slowly.

"I'm a born adventurer, señor," Diego answered. "I've been places no other penguin has been before! I've been all around the world. I've come from Miami… what a beautiful place! Drinking cocktails and lying in the sun!"

Ray's eyes grew wider as he gasped, "Lying in the sun…?"

"Si, amigo! Lying in paradise! But someone must have slipped something in my drink! One minute I'm in paradise then the next thing I know I'm in and out of consciousness inside a cage," Diego explained.

"You poor thing" said Nayha, holding a hand to her heart as she shook her head.

"Señorita, it was tragic. But as tragic as it was at least it led me to your beautiful eyes," winked Diego.

Nayha looked down to her feet with a small giggle, but not before Clyde noticed her cheeks slightly redden with the compliment. He turned away from his friend and looked hard at Diego in a disapproving manner.

"It's going to be tough to leave that life behind me in Miami… the beaches, the brunches, the music, the dancing, the sun," Diego continued, having captured the full attention of every resident on Penguin Beach.

"Never let him go…" Preston whispered conspiratorially to Nayha which only infuriated Clyde more.

"If you would all be so kind to show me where I can rest, I would be most grateful. It has been a long journey and I need to come to terms with my new surroundings," explained Diego with a swift wave towards the expanse of Penguin Beach. Suddenly to Clyde, in that very moment, Penguin Beach felt very small.

"Of course," replied Arthur. "If you could all show our new friend to the cave while I talk to Clyde, that would be most helpful," he added.

The group, led by Anton (and Gary – who was now being introduced to Diego) took Diego to the cave by the pool where all the penguins slept. Clyde glared at Diego and Nayha talking and laughing with each other. The feeling of jealousy started to fuel Clyde. It wasn't a feeling he had felt before and he didn't like it one bit.

"So, what do you think Clyde?" asked Arthur with interest.

"I don't get the fascination, personally," Clyde muttered.

"Perhaps it's that Latin charm!" smirked Arthur.

"That'll wear off. This afternoon when it's showtime – he'll soon see who the star around here is," replied Clyde with his eyes still firmly locked on Diego.

It's a good job looks can't kill. Or Diego would be pushing up daisies.

TWO

When it came to feeding time it's fair to say that the penguins never said grace. In fact, it was more "On your marks, get set, go!" But there was always a routine with the feeding. When one of the zoo keepers threw the first fish towards the penguins Clyde was ALWAYS the first to leap above all the others and catch the fish, but this time would be very different.

As the fish was tossed in the air Clyde did his trademark leap towards it but then almost in slow motion something horrified him as he realised Diego was leaping with even higher velocity than he was, and had soon swallowed the fish in one gulp while in mid-air. As the two penguins began to head towards the ground

Clyde felt like he had been punched hard in the stomach. He was very embarrassed.

"Unbelievable!" Pam gasped "How did you ever learn to leap like that?" she asked.

"Ah, that was nothing," Diego smirked. "I can jump much higher – heights don't really bother me. I am an ex-paratrooper."

"Sometimes I wee in the pool!" Anton stated proudly.

Nayha smiled at Diego. "Wow Diego – that's pretty impressive!"

"I use to free fall from ten thousand feet," Diego added.

"Amazing!" Nayha gasped as Clyde rolled his eyes.

"One day my parachute didn't open at all," Diego said causing another gasp from Nayha. "I saw my life flash before my eyes but luckily an eagle soared down and I glided on his back to safety. I owe that bird my life," Diego explained.

"Well that was lucky." Clyde muttered sarcastically.

"Weren't you scared?" asked Nayha.

"Luckily after my training I'm unable to feel fear anymore," Diego said.

"I'm a bit like that," Preston butted in. "I mean, I've always done well under pressure."

"What?! You near enough had an emotional breakdown last night! You completely snapped at me!" mentioned Pierce.

"Well when I'm overcome by the powerful Titanic soundtrack - you don't simply tell me to 'grow a pair!' The ship went down but their love lasts forever!" Preston whimpered.

Yohann snorted in disgust at all the penguins before drawing his attention to Diego. "I must say, monsieur, I always pictured paratroopers to be much, much taller."

"Yeah well maybe he was once six foot three, but had a bad landing," Clyde smirked which caused all the penguins to chuckle slightly.

"And I suppose, señor, you have many adventures to share with your comrades?" Diego asked while staring daggers at Clyde.

A moment of silence hit Penguin Beach as all the penguins turned their attention to Clyde.

"I didn't think so," Diego smirked. "I've travelled the world – and been to places you can only dream of, from Hollywood to Hawaii!"

"Others always say to me that I belong in Hawaii," Preston muttered proudly.

"Who?" asked Pierce.

"Others," replied Preston.

"What others?" Pierce questioned.

"You don't know them," Preston answered.

"Hawaii would be paradise," Ray sighed.

"Oh, come on, you guys – please tell me you aren't seriously buying this, are you?" Clyde shouted. "This guy is just like us – a completely normal penguin!"

"Would a 'normal penguin' hike the most dangerous trail in the world on Mount Huashan in China?" Diego bragged.

"Incredible!" gasped Arthur.

"That's nothing – I once rode bareback on a great white shark!" Diego added.

"You've ridden a great white?" Bobby gasped.

"I once pooped in a bucket!" yelled Anton.

'Seriously guys – don't buy this garbage. It's showtime soon and let's remember that the visitors come to see an amazing show. Sure, the star might be me but we all do our bit. Maybe

then Mr Hotshot over here will realise actions speak louder than words… the visitors won't want to be bored to death with his made-up stories," Clyde smirked.

The penguins then started to prepare for their performance.

Clyde noticed strange goings on outside Penguin Beach – the zoo keepers looked like they were putting up posters and displays of Diego all around the beach to attract people. There seemed to be more of a crowd gathering around Penguin Beach than usual. Clyde didn't like what he was seeing – not one bit.

Preston started fixing up Nayha's hair and it wasn't too long before Pierce approached them both.

"I'm not happy with you," Preston told Pierce. "Please don't embarrass me like that again. I'll have you know many have told me I scream Hawaii."

"Okay sorry." Pierce replied before turning his attention to Nayha.

"Would you like me to fix up your hair sweetie?" Pierce said to her which Preston was not pleased about at all – since he had just spent some time working on her hair.

"I didn't realise her hair was broken," Preston said bluntly, while Nayha looked incredibly awkward as she was stuck in the middle of them both debating over her hair.

- X -

Ray was in the cave making coffee before the performance. Clyde had joined him, marvelling as ever over Ray's systematic coffee making before every show, not to mention the wonderful way he made it. No other penguin on Penguin Beach had quite the same coffee-making skills as Ray.

"You do make the best coffee, Ray," complimented Clyde as Ray handed him a steaming cup.

"Yes, I do, don't I?" said Ray. "I just love the feeling of warmth the kettle gives. It's one of the few things that brings me pleasure in life."

Arthur approached them, waddling over. "Ray please be careful with what containers you use for drinks today. I hate to say it but Anton's been urinating in things again," Arthur told him reluctantly.

"I know," replied Ray, "some of our stuff was absolutely full of pee! But don't worry I moved them all out of the way,"

"That's a relief," Arthur replied before waddling away. Yohann then made his way over.

"I need coffee," Yohann snorted at Ray.

"Oh okay, sure," stuttered Ray, "how do you take it?"

"Black... like my soul," Yohann answered.

Yohann grabbed some coffee that was half-hidden on the back table and took a huge gulp.

"Ahhhhh," he sighed in relief, "that's more like it. That apple juice I found earlier was absolutely horrible..." Yohann said as he trotted off. Both Clyde and Ray stared at one another aghast.

"That wasn't Anton's...?" said Clyde slowly.

"Yes," gulped Ray. "Best not to mention it."

The crowd started to gather around Penguin Beach. The visitors couldn't wait to see the penguins perform for them.

Anton opened the show as he ran around the pool like a lunatic many times with Gary attached to him. They were diving in and out of the pool countless times within the first minute! This of course got a lot of laughs from the enchanted audience.

The crowd watched on as some of the other penguins performed impressive dives and swam in unison together, as well as going over to the visitors to greet them.

Then Clyde was ready for his big finale – he was ready to give them his Irish dancing routine which had delighted audiences for years. He performed proudly. He jumped out in front of the crowd and started to perform his trademark routine that had made him so popular, but it wasn't long before the audience turned their attention behind him.

Diego was performing backflips, front flips and every kind of flip you could think of, right behind Clyde. The crowd had never seen anything like it in their lives.

"Please welcome London Zoo's newest star penguin - Diego!" a voice called out from the speakers around Penguin Beach.

The crowd went crazy for Diego and as the cheers grew louder and louder, Clyde's heart sank lower and lower.

It was becoming increasingly apparent to Clyde that Penguin Beach wasn't big enough for the two of them.

THREE

As the sun set over the zoo that evening, Clyde stood alone watching Diego showboating to the other penguins, who were certainly enjoying the entertainment. All except Yohann, of course. The only thing he ever seemed to enjoy was being miserable. He approached Clyde as he screwed up his face in disapproval at the others.

"How did it change so quickly?" Clyde muttered to himself. He couldn't believe how the dynamics of Penguin Beach had changed so drastically in less than twenty-four hours.

"Whatever happens in life, you deserve it," Yohann stated with a sigh.

"You can see through it, can't you? It's all an act," said Clyde.

"So what if it is? What are you going to do about it?" replied Yohann. "All you dancing penguins are all the same. All beak with no peck. In France, we are smarter than that, we make sure situations are dealt with… and then we paint," he added.

Clyde thought hard before starting to approach the other penguins.

"Well? Where are you going?" Yohann called.

"To peck." Clyde muttered to himself.

Clyde approached the group as Diego was telling them more adventure stories about

himself. It seemed like he was just coming to the end of one.

"...then after saving her life, Her Majesty offered me a knighthood but of course I turned it down. I just did what anyone would have done in that situation – saved the Queen of England!" said Diego.

"You'd think she'd be more careful, skiing at her age," Pam said in shock.

"Pretty impressive," smiled Nayha. "So you're quite the tough guy, hey?" she added, which caused Clyde's blood to boil – not easy when you're a penguin.

"Well. I don't mean to brag, but I'm quite the tough guy myself," said Preston.

"Seriously?" interrupted Pierce. "I think I've seen you cry during every Julie Andrews movie there is," he added.

"Pierce, I'm not a robot, she's a genius, the woman could play Batman!" Preston replied sternly.

"Guys," Clyde interrupted, "do you mind if I talk to Diego privately for a minute?"

"Ooooooooohhhh, I feel tension," Preston flapped.

"Let's give these two some space," said Arthur, as he guided the group away so Clyde and Diego could talk alone.

"Yes?" asked Diego cautiously.

"Look Diego, I feel we got off on the wrong foot. I'm kinda used to things being a certain way around here. I mean, no one likes change, right? I was just hoping we could start again and get along?" Clyde explained.

"Sure?" Diego replied.

"That's good, I mean, I should understand more, really. It must be so hard for you being here," said Clyde.

"What?" asked Diego.

"Oh – it's just, after hearing about all your adventures, I've never known a penguin with such freedom. The world was your oyster; 'Diego the explorer'... 'the many adventures of Diego' – but now what, hey? You are going to be with us for perhaps the rest of your life. Dancing and

performing at the click of somebody's fingers. I mean, us lot are used to it… it's what we know. Y'know, being prisoners; we've made this our home. But I mean, someone like you that's used to being free? Wow. That must be really hard. I mean, I'm not sure how I'd be able to cope. I'd probably be making a break for it personally, but hey that's just me! I'm sure you'll get used to it. I mean, who needs beaches and cocktails in the sun when you can have the flashes of camera and children throwing popcorn at you daily? You'll learn to love it! Anyway, see you tomorrow at showtime!" Clyde said as he waddled away.

Diego was left on his own, deep in thought. In his head he could hear the jeers of the crowd, he could see the flashing of cameras – it suddenly hit home that he was trapped and a prisoner.

To Diego, the outside world looked a lot more appealing and satisfying. "What am I doing here?" Diego muttered to himself. He needed to get away.

FOUR

As it got later, just before the penguins retreated to go to sleep, Arthur was doing his usual roll call to make sure everyone was present and accounted for. There started to be quite the panic when the penguins realised that Diego was missing.

"Diego? Diego!?" Arthur called out.

"We've looked every…" Bobby said, before being immediately interrupted by Pam.

"We've looked everywhere," said Pam.

"Where could he be?" Nayha said with worry.

Clyde was feeling nauseous as Yohann was staring a hole through him.

"He couldn't have gotten too far… it's so cold out there," Ray mumbled.

"Do you think he hated me?" Preston wept to Pierce.

"Something's not right," muttered Arthur.

"I know! I've lost Gary!" panicked Anton. "Gary?! Gary?!" he cried.

"Oh, give it a rest, you guys. Face it – Diego's gone! He's a penguin that explores the world. He was never going to want to stay here. He was always going to make an escape for it the first chance he could. This was always going to happen," Clyde stated.

A look of realisation suddenly hit Arthur's face. "Clyde, you were the last one to see and talk with Diego. What did he say?" Arthur asked.

"That's right ... we left him with you last," said Pierce.

"Which was probably the worst call since they cast Pierce Brosnan in Mamma Mia," added Preston.

"You really need to let that go," sighed Pierce.

"Hold on! Let me handle this," called out Yohann with a very aggressive French tone. "It was apparent to everyone that the second Diego arrived, Clyde became a ticking time bomb. Overcome by jealousy, anger and resentment slowly consumed him more and more before he finally snapped, striking Diego to death as he slept. I'm afraid, my friends, that Diego is now sleeping with the fishes!" he explained.

"Of course not! He's just left, that's all!" replied Clyde.

"Left?" Bobby gulped. "But that's suicide! He'll never make it out of the zoo on his own!"

"Clyde, what do you mean?" Asked Nayha.

"Okay look, I may have hinted to Diego there wasn't much for him here. I guess he thought he was better off away from Penguin Beach," explained Clyde.

"He could die out there!" cried Pam.

"Clyde, you know how dangerous it is for a penguin to be alone in the zoo and how vulnerable we are outside here," Arthur said sternly.

"Gary? Gary?!" called Anton.

"Oh, come on. You heard all his stories, right? He'll be fine out there. He's probably made it out of the zoo already," assured Clyde.

"What have you done?" Yohann said, as he shook his head disapprovingly.

"You're the one that said I should do something!" cried Clyde.

"I meant with a threat! I'm French!" yelled Yohann.

"I found Gary! I was holding him the whole time," Anton chuckled. "Wait - who are we looking for again?" he asked.

Nayha gave Clyde a disappointed look.

"You could have sent him to his death - and for what?" she asked.

"Nayha please, I..." Clyde tried to explain before she turned her back on him.

"I don't know who you are anymore," she said as she walked with the rest of the group into the cave.

Clyde sighed. Although at the time he thought he was doing the right thing, all he felt now was disappointment, stupidity and guilt. He knew he somehow had to make it right. He could see a hole under the fence where it was apparent Diego had most likely escaped from.

"Well… here goes nothing," Clyde sighed to himself.

FIVE

Clyde was outside Penguin Beach looking around at the zoo surroundings.

"Which way would he have gone?" Clyde muttered to himself, before slowly waddling to the toilets. "Maybe he needed to go before the long journey," Clyde thought to himself. But after a long check in the toilets, sadly there was no Diego to be seen.

As Clyde waddled out of the toilets he heard the sounds of cackling towards his right. Swirling his head, he saw two hyenas howling with laughter from inside their cage.

The two male hyenas were named Snicker and Heckle and seemed to be apart from the other hyenas in their cage. This was because the other hyenas found their constant jokes and

laughing so annoying that they were made to separate themselves away from the others.

"A penguin all alone going to the toilet – that's not something you see every day, hey Heckle?" Snicker laughed.

"Hey Snicker, have you heard the poem of the penguin going to the toilet? It goes like this:

Alone he sits broken hearted

Tried to poo but only…?"

"That's enough of that!" Clyde called out before standing directly in front of the hyena cage.

"That's brilliant!" howled Snicker. "Genius!" he added. "How about this one? What do you call a penguin in the middle of the zoo with nowhere to go?"

"What?" Asked Heckle.

"Lost!" Snicker replied before both he and Heckle snapped their sharp teeth at Clyde. They may have both been idiots and acting like fools but they were still very dangerous, especially to a penguin. Clyde was very happy there was a cage separating them.

"You know, Snicker, I think this might be a different penguin," Heckle stated.

"I think you're right, Heckle. This one looks different. Who'd have thought it – two penguins on offer," replied Snicker.

"That must have been Diego! Where did he go? Did he say anything?" asked Clyde.

"Oh nothing – he just gave us the COLD shoulder," Snicker answered before him and Heckle started to howl with laughter once again.

"Please, it's important. He and I have had our differences lately and it's not safe for him to be out there. I need to get him back to Penguin Beach. Can you tell me which way he went?" Clyde pleaded.

"I guess they need to 'break the ice'!" Heckle snorted as he and Snicker continued to howl with laughter.

"I got one, I got one!" Snicker interrupted. "If they were struggling to make decisions together, maybe they should 'flipper coin,'" Snicker joked before continuing to roll on the floor laughing.

"They always say it's difficult for penguins to get along with each other… always FISHING for compliments," Heckle added before the hyenas continued laughing their heads off.

Clyde rolled his eyes.

"Thanks anyway…" he sighed before continuing his journey, determined to find Diego.

"I hope you find what you need to 'igloo' your relationship back together!" Snicker snorted as Clyde walked deeper into the zoo.

SIX

Benjamin Blacker was a very complicated man. He was quite short, with bright orange frizzy hair, freckles scattered all across his face and a huge gap between his two front teeth. He was in his late thirties and was known for his short temper. He paced up and down in his underground lair, addressing his two associates Denzel Driscoll, a tall, scrawny-looking man with a long pointy nose and gangly long legs and Norris Bishop, a short round man, whose personal hygiene was horrific. He smelt like a sauna filled with hundreds of cheeseburgers abandoned for months, because Norris was so incredibly unhealthy he was constantly sweating. Even standing up from a chair would break him into a sweat.

Both Denzel and Norris were a thieving partnership. They had stolen many things in their lifetime, from robbing banks to stealing prize-winning cows. You name it, they stole it.

"Gentlemen, tonight is a defining night in the life of Benjamin Blacker. Tonight, I put my name back on the map, with this very unique heist," Benjamin explained to them like a Sergeant Major addressing his troops.

He clicked a button to present a picture on his projector.

"Behold, gentlemen! This little guy is the answer to my prayers," Benjamin pointed at the projection, causing Denzel and Norris to look at each other and the projected image, plainly confused. They were staring at a picture of a penguin with what appeared to be a mohawk on its head.

"You called us here just to get a bloomin' penguin?" Denzel asked, startled.

"You told us this job was BIG!" Norris added sternly.

"The biggest job of our lives you said," Denzel said.

"Oh, but it is gentlemen. This is just not any penguin. Allow me to present just what this…"

Just as Benjamin was about to launch into an explanation to his two associates, the lair door opened and he was interrupted.

"Benji, sweetie, would you and your friends like any fizzy orange? I just made a batch," a sweet old lady said, turning on a light which revealed Benjamin's dark lair to be nothing more than a basement. The sweet old lady was Mrs Blacker, Benjamin's mother.

"Hello boys," Mrs Blacker smiled at both Denzel and Norris.

"Hello Mrs Blacker," they both muttered reluctantly, although as politely as possible.

"Mum, what are you doing?!" Benjamin yelled in frustration.

"I just thought you and your friends might be thirsty, Benji," Mrs Blacker smiled at her son.

"You're so embarrassing!" Benjamin cried out. "We are in a super serious meeting. You don't drink fizzy orange at super serious meetings!"

"Well, are you sure, dear?" Mrs Blacker asked.

"Yes, I'm…we don't want…ugh! Ah! Ugh! You're so annoying!" Benjamin screamed in frustration, too angry to even speak clearly.

"Okay, well you boys have fun now – let me know if you change your mind," Mrs Blacker said, as she started to leave the basement.

"Turn the light off!" Benjamin replied to her sternly.

"What was that, dearie?" Mrs Blacker asked sweetly.

"TURN THE LIGHT OFF!" Benjamin screamed.

"WHAT was that, dearie?" Mrs Blacker repeated but this time in a disapproving tone, as she glared at her son. This look made Benjamin very aware he was on thin ice with his mother.

"Could you please turn the light off?" Benjamin asked reluctantly, in a more well-mannered tone.

"Of course, Benji," Mrs Blacker replied, before turning the light off and leaving the basement.

Denzel and Norris looked awkwardly at Benjamin; they felt a bit embarrassed for him.

But Benjamin, ever the professional, went back to addressing them in a far more powerful, sinister tone, as if the interruption had never happened.

"Gentlemen! Tonight, this penguin puts us on the map! This penguin is the most famous penguin in the world! Allow me to show you the following video," Benjamin said as he pressed a button once again. A video appeared on the screen but it seemed like it was taking an awfully long time to load.

"Is this it?" Norris asked, as he scratched his head, puzzled.

"Why's it taking so long? It's not working?" Denzel asked.

"I don't believe it... it was working fine earlier," Benjamin muttered to himself before calling out to his mother.

"HEY, MUM!" He yelled.

"Yes, Benji?" a sweet little voice called back.

"Are you on the computer?" he asked.

"Oh yes! I'm watching some wonderful videos of kittens," she replied.

"Can you wait ten minutes please? It's making our connection slow down here!" Benjamin explained.

"Okay, sweetie!" Mrs Blacker called back.

Benjamin then went back to his sinister tone of voice.

"Gentlemen, please watch this incredible penguin at work," he continued before pressing the button to play the video.

The video was a promotional video from London Zoo. It showed clips of all the amazing performances the mohawk penguin had been involved in – all of his tricks, stunts and dances were caught in a short highlights video. It showed audiences from all over the world travelling to see him perform.

"I feel I need say no more," Benjamin said as the video ended.

"But why a penguin?" Denzel asked.

"Because that penguin will be part of my new and unique act; BENJAMIN BLACKER AND THE DAREDEVIL PENGUIN! This bird is now London Zoo's biggest attraction but, once I get my hands on it, I'll have one of the biggest animal attractions on the planet! We will travel the world! People will come pouring in from every corner of the globe to see us! Gentlemen, not only will I pay you handsomely for your help in retrieving me this penguin but once this penguin is in our grasp there'll be no stopping us. We will buy or steal the biggest animal attractions in the world and pass them off as our own. You'll be a part of my childhood dream of making that a reality. You will be a part of 'Benjamin Blacker's Supreme Circus!' The likes of which the world has never seen! Gentlemen, we will be millionaires," Benjamin added in a dramatic finish.

The word 'millionaires' made both Denzel and Norris' eyes light up with glee. It was almost like they could see the pound and dollar signs directly in front of them.

"Pounds," Denzel muttered to himself.

"Dollars," Norris smiled.

"We'll have banks," said Denzel.

"Full of cash," Norris added.

"Quids," Denzel smirked.

"Bucks," mumbled Norris.

"The biggest shares!" yelled Denzel.

"MILLIONAIRES!" cried Norris.

"Millions," mouthed Denzel.

"In truckloads," Norris added, as he licked his lips and rubbed his grimy hands together in excitement.

Benjamin smirked at Denzel and Norris' reactions – it appeared they were on board.

"Gentlemen, let's put this plan into action. I've been planning this for some time. Follow my lead," Benjamin ordered, before his mum once again poked her head into the basement.

"Anyone for cookies?" she asked.

SEVEN

Back in the cave at Penguin Beach everyone was still mortified with Clyde.

"I'm just so worried about Diego," Nayha whimpered. "Why was Clyde so stupid?"

Preston and Pierce tried to comfort her.

"He'll be okay," smiled Pierce.

"Yeah I'm sure right now he's setting off to some exotic beach somewhere for sun, sea and relaxation," Preston added.

"Thanks guys," Nayha smiled. "I'm going to have to go outside and talk to Clyde. I need to know what drove him to this."

As she left the cave, she couldn't help overhearing Pierce and Preston's quiet, passing remarks.

"You know Preston. I'm really proud of you

making Nayha feel better," she heard Pierce say.

"Thanks, it seemed the right thing to do, as he's definitely dead," replied Preston's low voice.

"Ahh," said Pierce.

Nayha's heart sank, trying not to imagine such a dreadful thing. But it was realising that there was no Clyde to be found outside that caused her to panic even more.

Nayha quickly rushed back into the cave. "Clyde's gone!" she yelled.

"What?" cried Arthur.

"He's nowhere to be seen!" said Nayha.

"He must have gone after Diego," said Pierce.

"What do we ..." Bobby was about to say, before being interrupted by his wife Pam. "What do we do?" she asked.

"What if he felt guilt-ridden and felt he needed to leave too?" Nayha said worryingly. "I'm going out there. I'm going to bring them both back," she added.

"No Nayha. It's not safe," Arthur said sternly.

"I need to do this," replied Nayha.

"We can't lose anymore penguins," said Arthur. "You won't survive out there alone".

"Well then, me and Pierce are coming with you," said Preston.

"Oh - thanks for volunteering me," said Pierce.

"Well, she's not going out there alone!" replied Preston. "I mean, obviously Bobby and Pam should stay here together," he added.

"Do we have to?" Bobby said, as he glared at Pam.

"And Arthur can't come - he has more wrinkles than Downton Abbey... no offence," Preston said, "and Ray would just moan the entire time!" he added.

"What about Anton?" asked Pierce.

Preston looked at Pierce sarcastically as if he was shocked Pierce was seriously suggesting that.

"Anton? We want someone that will be able to protect Nayha! Besides, Nayha is going through a lot right now and needs someone she can talk to. Anton has about two conversations within him."

"I'm a tree!" yelled Anton.

"And that's the good one," Preston pointed out.

"Okay, I suppose I could come with you and Nayha. It's just… wait a minute - where's Yohann?" said Pierce.

EIGHT

Clyde had been searching the zoo for a while and waddling around the zoo was tiresome work for a penguin. As he searched the reptile house he decided he needed a small break. Just on cue as Clyde decided on this, he noticed a pit of sand in the middle of the reptile house.

"Perfect!" Clyde thought to himself as he hopped over a small barrier and slid down into the pit before nestling himself in the warm sand.

"Ray would be sooooo jealous," Clyde thought to himself as he slowly began to nod off and get his forty winks. Little did Clyde know there were two sinister red eyes staring at him as he slept.

A twenty-foot long Burmese python began to slither its way over, hissing softly.

"What a wonderful treat," the python whispered to himself. "I can't remember the last time I had a midnight snack." The python began to contemplate just how to tackle the sleeping penguin and how to eat him.

"Down in one gulp would be such a waste for such a tasty, plump little penguin," the python began to ponder as he slowly began to circle Clyde.

"So tender and fresh – so delicioussssss," the python hissed, as he licked his lips and began to grip Clyde with his long body.

Clyde opened his eyes but before he had the chance to run he realised he was completely in

the snake's grasp. He couldn't even move his flippers.

"It's your wake-up call," the snake jeered.

"Thanks," Clyde began to say in panic. "I don't believe we've been formally introduced," Clyde continued, as he tried his best to wiggle out of the python's grasp. "I'm Clyde!"

"Pleasure," the snake chuckled.

"What's your name?" Clyde asked, trying to buy himself as much time as he could.

"Oh that's not important," the python hissed as he began to lick his lips even more.

"Oh I think so," replied Clyde. "I think it's only courtesy, since we are seemingly quite close to one another right now."

"I said it's not important!" The snake snapped, appearing very frustrated.

"Apologies," Clyde replied. "You know, I'm truly sorry if I've intruded into your home in any way. My mistake! We're not always in our right minds when we're tired. I'll just be on my way as soon as you let me go, hey?" Clyde said with a nervous chuckle.

"On the contrary, you're right on cue," the python hissed.

Clyde's heart was beating at an alarming rate. He was looking around trying to find something, anything he could use to his advantage. He noticed a sign just outside the snake pit with the words 'Cuddles – Burmese Python' on it.

"Cuddles? Who's that?" Clyde asked.

"No one!" The python barked.

"Wait," Clyde said with a chuckle, "It's you, isn't it? You're Cuddles? Like … your name is Cuddles?!" Clyde began to laugh.

"I had no choice in the matter!" Cuddles snapped.

"Woah! Calm down," replied Clyde. "Do you need a hug?" He added, chortling.

"Do you not realise what danger you are in, you fool?! And what's about to happen to you?" Cuddles warned.

"Well, I was worried at first but it's obvious all you really wanted was a cuddle!" Clyde laughed.

"ENOUGH!" yelled Cuddles, as he used his incredible strength to start squeezing Clyde tightly.

Clyde faced his apparent doom as he was flung closer and closer to the jaws of Cuddles. He started to regret deeply what he had done to Diego and just hoped that Diego was safe. Just as Clyde was about to hit the tip of Cuddles' tongue a heroic moment occurred in the nick of time – a French heroic moment!

Out of nowhere, Yohann had leapt down into the snake pit and right on top of the snake's mouth which caused an almighty collision between Clyde, Yohann and Cuddles' head. Clyde and Yohann were slung into the sand of the snake pit as Cuddles regained his composure.

"Yohann?!" Clyde called out. "You saved me!"

"I regret it already!" Yohann snorted, as Cuddles glared at them both.

"Now I'm really mad!" Cuddles hissed before launching his jaws at Yohann. Clyde quickly darted towards them, pushing himself and Yohann out of the way of Cuddles' mouth, leaving the python to receive a mouth full of sand.

"I didn't need you..." Yohann ignorantly grunted as Cuddles recovered. Clyde looked at him, unimpressed.

Yohann reluctantly sighed, "Saved by the Irish... no one must ever know about this."

"Its fine - we're even," Clyde smiled.

"Okay - well what do we do?" Yohann asked.

"Didn't you have a plan before leaping in here?" Clyde asked.

"I'm French! We leap first and ask questions later," Yohann proudly replied.

Clyde noticed a long stick on the ground by Yohann. He picked it up quickly before showing Yohann.

"Yes, let's hit him with a stick. That's exactly what we need to do." Yohann replied sarcastically.

"It's not to hit him with!" shouted Clyde, "it's to..."

But before he had the chance to explain, both Clyde and Yohann had to dart out of the way as Cuddles lunged at them once again.

"Yohann, distract him!" Clyde yelled as he hid behind a rock in the pit.

"I'll distract him whilst you hide? Typical Irishmen!" Yohann replied as he dived out of the way once again from another lunge by the python.

"Lead him in my direction!" Clyde shouted.

"Your funeral," Yohann sighed, before making a dart towards the rock that Clyde was behind.

Cuddles' eyes locked onto Yohann, as the French penguin ran as quickly as he could. Cuddles smiled.

"Dead end … literally," he hissed to himself before making a ginormous leap towards Yohann. Cuddles' mouth was the widest it had been and looked like he would swallow Yohann whole, but out jumped Clyde and he bravely wedged a stick right in between the huge jaws of Cuddles. Cuddles once again slammed into the sand looking at the long stick wedged in his mouth.

Both Clyde and Yohann stood right in front of the

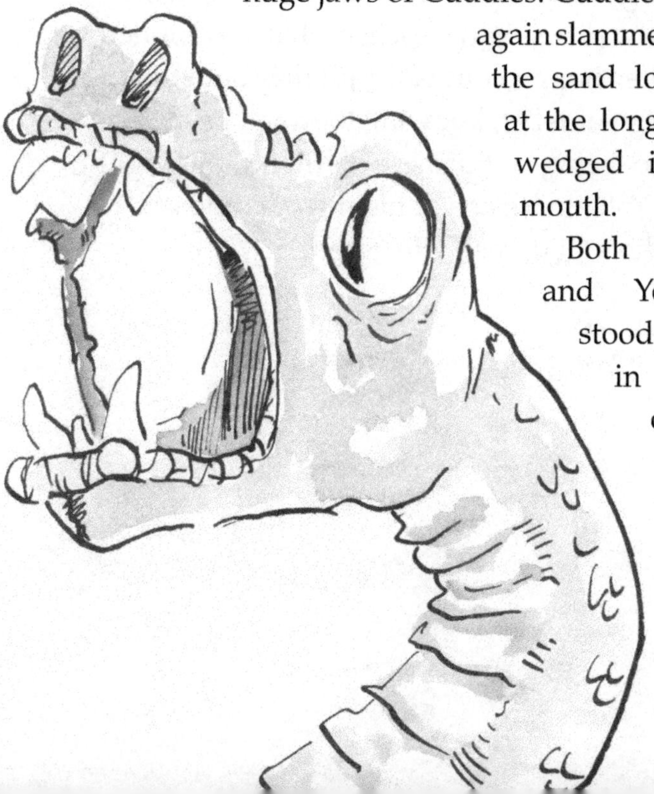

python as they watched him trying desperately to crush the stick that was lodged in his mouth.

"It worked!" Clyde said in shock. He had even surprised himself.

"HA – HA!" Yohann exclaimed before starting to mock Cuddles. "Look at you! Lying on the ground, fighting and struggling with nowhere to turn! How very much like life!" Yohann jeered.

There was a slight snapping noise, like the stick wouldn't hold out for much longer.

"I think that's our cue to get out of here … like right now," Clyde said assertively, before grabbing Yohann so they could climb their way out of the pit using the rockery that surrounded it. As they hopped out of the pit they both took a huge sigh of relief, knowing they had been very close to being a Burmese Python's midnight snack. Yohann looked at his surroundings.

"Who's Cuddles?" He asked.

NINE

Nayha, Preston and Pierce made their way into the zoo. The plan was to get everyone back to Penguin Beach together as soon as possible.

"All I'm saying is there's no way I'm not crying when we're all reunited and back home," said Preston.

"You cried as we left!" Pierce replied.

"That's not my fault! I'd just listened to 'True Colours'. I'm not made of stone, Pierce," Preston explained.

"Guys, please can we focus. I'm really worried. It looks like they may have gone deeper into the zoo. Who knows what they've all come face to face with," Nayha sighed, as she lowered her head.

"Stop worrying Nayha, they're all tough birds. You gotta believe in them," replied Pierce.

"Of course – have faith that they're okay!" smiled Preston.

Nayha smiled with a "Thanks guys" before waddling on. Once again, her companions' voices were not quite as quiet as they would have hoped.

"Definitely dead?" she heard Preston whispered to Pierce.

"Definitely," Pierce replied.

"You know Nayha, maybe going deeper into the zoo isn't such a great idea. Maybe we should go back to Penguin Beach? For all we know they could all be on their way back," Pierce called out to Nayha.

"If they had been heading back, we would have seen them by now," Nayha called back, hoping the despair she felt at their last words was not obvious in her voice. "We're not going back till we find them. We're family," she added.

Suddenly, she heard sniggering in the dark nearby.

It was Snicker and Heckle.

"Hey Heckle. It appears penguins are like London buses tonight! You wait what feels a lifetime for one and then they all show up at the same time," Snicker giggled.

"I think he might have seen the others!" said Preston.

"You think?" Pierce replied sarcastically.

"Snicker, we've seen too many penguins wandering around tonight, something seems very FISHY around here," Heckle howled as he and Snicker began to crack up.

Preston even giggled to himself, causing a look of disapproval from both Pierce and Nayha.

"What? I can't laugh at comedy gold?" said Preston.

"Could you tell us where they went?" asked Nayha. "It's really important we find them. They could be in severe danger," she added.

"Yes. Please help. One of them is new and from Spain. Have you seen him? He has a big ghettolicious kind of Mohawk going on," added Preston, which caused another disapproving look from Pierce.

"What? I thought it might be relevant." Preston said.

"Really? You thought 'ghettolicious' might be relevant?" Pierce questioned.

"Yeah, we've seen him," replied Heckle.

"We even know where he is," Snicker added.

"Where? Please tell us?" said Nayha.

"Well, before we tell you that, maybe there's something you could do for us?" said Snicker, as both he and Heckle grinned through their cage.

"And what's that?" asked Nayha; she was very suspicious about what the two hyenas had in mind.

"You know, I actually know the Duke and Duchess of Cambridge. If you help us I'm sure I can help you get recognised by royalty," Preston offered.

"Didn't they just point towards you and smile?" asked Pierce.

"We had immediate chemistry, you weren't there!" Preston snapped.

"We actually had something else in mind" hissed Heckle.

"You see, the other hyenas aren't as into comedy quite as much as us..." added Snicker

"They are tired of our jokes and make us stay at least 50 meters away from them at all times..." Heckle explained

"So it's clear what we need to do," said Snicker.

"Stop telling jokes?" Nayha suggested.

"What?!" Both hyenas gasped.

"Not tell jokes!?" Snicker asked, puzzled.

"We just need new material!" Heckle called out.

Nayha rolled her eyes in disbelief.

"The gift shop has a hilarious joke book. We see guests reading from it all the time." Snicker explained.

"Go and get it for us. We don't care how you get it, just get it! We'll then help you find your little friends," Heckle added.

Nayha and Pierce both sighed in frustration.

Preston on the other hand seemed quite excited.

"Shopping!" He giggled.

TEN

After leaving the reptile house, Clyde and Yohann were both waddling around the zoo trying to think where they could search for Diego next.

"Are you nervous for him?" Yohann asked.

"Well, I was certainly less worried before you gave me the 'fifty ways he could die' speech. What was the one about the balloon?" Clyde asked.

But before Yohann could answer, they both halted at something they had never seen before.

"What's that? Is it dangerous?" whispered Clyde.

"I don't know … but whatever it is, I don't trust it," replied Yohann.

Clyde and Yohann both looked down at a stray cat that seemed to be taking a nap. Its snores sounded like puffy gasps of air – the snuggled up cat had soon stolen Clyde's heart.

"It's so cute! Surely it's harmless enough," Clyde said as he started to approach the cat slowly.

"Clyde, walk away! I once knew a penguin who thought an elephant was cute. Let's just say it ended up as a pancake penguin!" Yohann warned.

"Stop thinking the worst in everyone and everything! Maybe it can help us. It might have seen Diego?" said Clyde.

"Or it could potentially stab you in the face," replied Yohann.

Clyde got closer to the cat and began to stroke it.

"See Yohann – there's absolutely nothing to be worried about … you should …" but before Clyde could finish his sentence an angry "MEOW" shriek rang out and before Clyde knew what had happened he was met with a humongous drop kick in the face by the cat.

"Why?!!?" Clyde yelled as the cat was in a ninja-like pose ready for battle, staring intensely at both Clyde and Yohann.

"Don't mess with me, mon ami – I must warn you I once wrestled an alligator. I won't tell you what happened but let's just say – I have its eyeball as a souvenir," Yohann warned.

"What do you want? You were trying to grab me! You weren't trying to make me bathe, right?" the cat asked.

"We just wanted your help…" Clyde said as he slowly stood himself back up.

The cat lowered her arms, unfolding her attack-like pose.

"You're asking for my help?" she asked.

"Well, I was about to before you kicked me in the face!" Clyde explained.

The cat looked startled.

"My help? No one's ever asked me for my help before," she muttered.

"I'm starting to think this is more trouble than it's worth," Yohann whispered to Clyde.

"I'm Clyde, this is Yohann. We're two penguins from Penguin Beach. We were wondering if you could help us fi..."

The cat interrupted with excitement, "Okay it's happening! It's actually happening! You are asking for my help? Ha – ha!" The cat cackled.

"She's crazy," Yohann muttered.

"Oh no, no sorry! Let me introduce myself. I'm Taddy! I guess I'm just shocked – no one has ever asked for my help before," she explained.

"Shocking!" Yohann replied, sarcastically.

"I've been a stray cat most of my life. I was abandoned as a kitten. The last few years it's just been me, myself and I! When I walk through the city all I am is an annoyance to people, or in the way. They kick me or shoo me away. At night I come here to sleep. I guess being around other animals makes me feel less lonely," Taddy sighed.

"Sadly, I left my violin at home," Yohann muttered to Clyde.

"But you've noticed me! It's been years and you've actually wanted to talk... not only that but you've asked for my help! I'm going to need a moment," Taddy said tearfully.

"Quick, while she's not looking, let's sneak away," Yohann suggested to Clyde but, before they could, Taddy soon turned her attention back to them.

"Okay, moment's over!" Taddy said excitedly. "How can I help? Gee, you have no idea how good that feels to say!" She added with glee.

"To be honest I'm not so sure if you can. We're looking for a friend of ours," explained Clyde.

"Friend?" Yohann asked, puzzled.

"Another penguin; spiky hair, exotic, Spanish accent?" Clyde added, as Taddy looked deep in thought. The more Taddy began to ponder, the more Clyde felt Taddy couldn't help them.

"It's okay. I thought it was a long shot," Clyde sighed as he and Yohann began to waddle away.

"But I've seen him!" Taddy called out, "I know exactly where he is," she added.

"You do?" Clyde gasped with excitement.

"Sure I do!" replied Taddy enthusiastically. "Follow me!"

She began to trot her way into the heart of the zoo.

"Great, let's go!" said Clyde, but as he began to follow her, Yohann quickly pulled him back.

"What are you doing?" asked Clyde.

"How do we know we can we trust her?" queried Yohann.

"Yohann, you saw how excited she got when we asked for her help – why would she be lying?" asked Clyde.

"For attention!" Yohann bluntly replied.

"Well, I trust her," said Clyde.

"If there's one thing we French pride ourselves on, it's being an excellent judge of character!" Yohann stated.

"You said the Russian ice skating team in the Winter Olympics were all witches!" Clyde rebuked him.

"It was madness! Absolute witchcraft! Nobody could naturally move like that!" Yohann grunted. "How do we even know for sure this creature has seen Diego?" He added.

Taddy was obviously eavesdropping on their concerns as she answered back shouting,

"Because he showed me how many times he could backflip!"

Clyde looked at Yohann with a raised eyebrow.

"Okay, she saw him," Yohann reluctantly sighed as he and Clyde started to follow Taddy.

ELEVEN

Nayha, Preston and Pierce were on the roof of the zoo's gift shop.

"This feels wrong. I've never stolen anything before," Pierce said anxiously. "Have you?" he asked Preston.

"Only during our production of 'The Greatest Showman' last year when I stole the show," replied Preston causing Pierce to roll his eyes.

"Right ... so how do we get in?" Nayha asked.

"It's a shame we're not smaller – there's a small pipe just there, that would be perfect," Pierce pointed out.

Preston noticed a little squirrel rummaging about on the roof.

"Well, maybe this little guy could help us?" Preston suggested as he approached the squirrel.

"Hey there, friend!" Preston said, which caused the squirrel to turn around and face him.

"We were wondering if you'd be able to help us?" Pierce added.

It was clear that the squirrel was very young and couldn't talk, as he nervously pointed to himself.

"Yes, you!" smiled Preston. "We wondered if you could help us get into the gift shop. Could you get in through that pipe and open a window for us, please?" Preston asked.

The squirrel rubbed his fingers and thumb together.

"He's asking what's in it for him," Pierce said.

"Yes, thank you Pierce, I do realise that. Need I remind you who has been the beach's charade champion five times in a row now?" Preston replied before turning his attention back to the squirrel.

"We will bring you peanuts! Lots and lots of peanuts," Preston promised.

"Something else we're stealing from somewhere?" Pierce asked disapprovingly.

The squirrel didn't take much convincing after being promised peanuts and soon shot up the pipe to get into the gift shop.

"Why didn't we just tell the squirrel what we wanted and ask him to get it?" quizzed Nayha.

"Well y'know, I thought whilst we are here, we might want to take a look at a few things? See if anything catches our eye, have a browse… I wonder if they do novelty glasses," said Preston.

"Preston, we are not stealing anything other than that joke book! And why novelty glasses?" Pierce asked reluctantly.

"It's the one thing missing for my eighties fancy dress party in a couple of weeks; I'm going as Elton John!" Preston said proudly.

"Can we just focus on the matter in hand, guys?" Nayha interrupted, before looking through a window to see if the squirrel was in the shop. As they all gathered around the window below them, they bowed their heads to see through it. They noticed the squirrel scurrying across the shop floor and looking up at the window at them.

"Well done, little guy! Now come up here and open up this window for us," Preston instructed.

The squirrel leapt onto one of the shelves in the gift shop. As he approached the latch to open the window he looked at the three penguins and once again rubbed his fingers and thumb together.

"Yes, don't worry. We will bring you peanuts," Pierce promised.

"AND ICE CREAM!" Preston called out.

"Ice cream now?" Pierce asked.

"Pierce, can't you see I'm negotiating?" Preston replied, before the squirrel unlatched the window so the penguins could make their way in.

"Let's just get this stupid thing" Pierce murmured, before hopping into the gift shop with the squirrel.

Preston was the next to make his way into the gift shop. As he dived into the opening there seemed to be a problem. He appeared to be stuck in the gap.

Pierce looked up at the window and saw the front half of Preston's body dangling from it.

"Brilliant." Pierce muttered.

The squirrel couldn't help but giggle at the situation.

Nayha's view, on the other hand, was far from pleasant. She was still on the roof and only had Preston's bum to stare at.

"Beautiful," she said to herself sarcastically.

"Well, this is embarrassing," Preston stated.

"For who? You or me?" asked Pierce.

"I know you're judging me right now, Pierce, and shame on you. So what if I'm still holding onto some Christmas-time weight?" Preston said defensively.

"It's July, Preston." Pierce stated, causing the squirrel to laugh hysterically.

"Look Preston, I'm just going to get this joke book now. We don't have time to kid around. We'll figure out how to get you out shortly." Pierce added before shouting up to Nayha.

"I'm going for the book, Nayha! Be right back!"

"Okay - hurry! I'm finding it really hard not to mess with Preston right now!" she shouted back.

"You're leaving me stuck here?" Preston screamed.

"Just for a few minutes. Stop being such a drama queen!" Pierce replied back as he ventured into the shop.

There were a few minutes of tense, awkward silence as Pierce disappeared and Nayha continued staring at the enormous backside of Preston who began whistling as he dangled to pass the time. Eager to distract herself from this uncomfortable sight, she spotted a few items on the top of the roof, obviously chucked there for storage by the shop staff; a lightbulb popped off in her head. Being a creative type of penguin, the idea of decorating Preston's enormous bottom, which now resembled a big, blank, round canvass to her, was suddenly very appealing.

"Bingo!" Pierce called out moments later from inside the shop.

"Have you got it?" Preston cried.

"Yes, I've got it" Pierce called back. "One Hundred Zoo Jokes!"

"Great, now get me out of here right now! Nayha, I know you're decorating my behind back there!" Preston shouted as Nayha began to laugh. After swiftly gathering the items from the top of the roof, she had spent the last few minutes making Preston's bottom look like a snowman.

"Nayha, how about you try pulling Preston back out from your side?" Pierce loudly suggested.

After a few attempts at pulling Preston out, Nayha couldn't make him budge.

"No luck," she called back out to Pierce. "You're going to have to push him through.".

Easier said than done. The window latch was right next to the ceiling with only a few shelves next to it.

"I'd need to dive off the shelves to try and push him through," Pierce said. "Squirrel, can you lend a hand? Stay very still Preston, we'll get you out in just a second."

"Well hurry up because if I have to keep staring directly at that elephant soft toy for much longer I will snap," Preston yelled.

"Oh come on. It's not th…"

"I will snap!" Preston screamed.

"Just stay cool," Pierce replied.

"I'm always cool."

Pierce and the squirrel climbed up the shelves by the window latch and were now at the top of them.

"Okay Preston, are you ready?" Pierce called up to him.

"Wait, what are you doing to do?" Preston asked as he saw the squirrel hop onto Pierce's back; they looked like they were preparing to leap.

"This might hurt but just for a second. Then you'll be free as a bird!" Pierce assured him.

"Hurt?" Preston asked, puzzled. "Pierce, why are you smiling?"

"I'm not," Pierce quickly replied. "It must be nerves," he added.

Nayha watched with bated breath, catching a brief glimpse of the rather gleeful expression on Pierce's face and shrewdly wondering if he was secretly enjoying the prospect of giving Preston a massive kick in the face. It wouldn't surprise her; the two were always bickering.

"Okay, well I trust you!" Preston called out.

"Don't make this harder than it needs to be!" Pierce called back.

Pierce took a huge deep breath before taking a huge leap towards Preston, his foot out in front of him with the little squirrel clutching hard on his back whilst holding the joke book.

"AHHHHHHHHHHHH!" Preston screamed before Pierce's foot met his face – the force of the leap and the momentum sent them flying through the window and back outside. They soared through the air and hit the ground next to the gift shop.

"OW!" Preston yelped.

"Wow – that was a thrill! My heart … phew," Pierce sighed.

"What heart?" Preston said bluntly.

"I said I'd get you out!" Pierce answered back.

Nayha called down to them from the roof of the gift shop. "If you guys have finished, let's

hurry up and get that book to those laughing fleabags and find the others," she said.

"What about him?" Pierce asked as he pointed to the little squirrel.

The squirrel was looking up at the penguins with puppy dog-like eyes – it was clear he wanted to stay with his new penguin friends.

"We can bring your peanuts and ice cream to you soon; just be sure to stop by Penguin Beach," Preston assured him.

"Y'know, I think he wants to stay with us…" Nayha stated.

"Do you?" Preston asked the squirrel, to which the squirrel nodded in excitement.

"Awww, that's so cute. Well we need to give you some form of name," Pierce suggested.

"Any ideas?" he asked the group.

"Nutz," Preston said proudly, which the squirrel seemed more than happy with.

They made their way back to the hyena cage to see Snicker and Heckle, handing them the joke book which both hyenas seemed thrilled with. They were in hysterics as they flicked through the pages in the book.

"There, you have your book. Now please tell us where our friends are," Nayha said sternly.

"Oh yeah … about that," Heckle giggled.

"There's been a slight change of plan," Snicker said, sinisterly.

Before they knew it, the penguins and their squirrel friend were grabbed from behind by very hairy arms. Nayha, Pierce and Preston and even the squirrel had been captured … but who by?

TWELVE

The smell from the sewer was revolting. But that didn't stop Benjamin Blacker and his associates Denzel Driscoll and Norris Bishop slowly making their way through the vile, repugnant and appalling stench.

"This is too much!" wailed Norris before briefly stopping for the third time to have a gagging fit.

"Shut your pie hole!" snapped Denzel, plodding grimly behind Benjamin and shoving Norris forward.

After their meeting at Benjamin's house, they had spent hours devising ways to break into the zoo undetected. They discussed posing as visitors and holding everyone at gunpoint while busting the penguin out – but the risk of being caught was too great. They discussed hiding in the zoo until dark to find a way to break out the penguin, but this was firmly refused by Norris whose paranoid thoughts about lions and tigers breaking loose at night and eating him were too much to handle. They discussed killing the zoo keepers themselves and pretending to be them, but that was near-impossible to achieve, considering the other zoo staff would know they were not who they said they were.

Then Benjamin latched onto the ingenious idea of crawling through the sewers. He spent hours mulling over the sewers underneath

London and it wasn't long before he came up with a cunning route to take them straight into London Zoo.

"In we go, boys!" he'd said, rubbing his hands gleefully. "Prepare yourselves for the greatest break-in of all time!"

Now, the smell from sewers is bad enough, but the smell from the sewer leading from a zoo is far more unpleasant. London Zoo was home to dozens of different animals and all the waste that the animals would go through during one day, including vomit and poop, would soon be dispatched into the sewer, which Benjamin, Denzel and Norris were now treading slowly through. They were up to their elbows in animal tripe! Benjamin was a lot more prepared; he had a very state-of-the-art gas mask strapped on his face, which left him unaffected by the atrocious smell. Denzel and Norris on the other hand didn't have quite the protection that Benjamin did. In fact, all they had was a peg each attached to their noses.

"He never mentioned a stroll through the sewer!" Norris continued complaining to Denzel as Benjamin walked ahead, looking this way and that.

"Stop moaning! It'll be worth it in the end. This is the most effective way to break into the zoo. The security will never see it coming!" Denzel explained

"Chances are they'll smell us..." Norris sighed

"Shut up!" snapped Denzel again.

"How much longer do we have to fight our way through all this!" Norris continued to moan. "If I see anymore straw floating on top of animal poop I think I'm going to scream!"

As Norris said this Benjamin stopped in his tracks and pointed at a huge pipe that was shovelling all the waste into the sewer. He signalled for them to make their way upwards.

"Not long now!" Denzel sniggered as he slapped Norris on the back.

Sadly, as Denzel did this it caused Norris to completely lose his balance and he ended up face-first in elephant poo.

THIRTEEN

"WELCOME ONE AND ALL TO P.G.T – THAT'S 'PRIMATES GOT TALENT!' THE ONLY CONTEST IN THE WORLD THAT CELEBRATES THE WONDERFUL DIFFERENT TALENTS US PRIMATES HAVE! I AM YOUR HOST, BOB BOONHOUSE!" The baboon announced to all the different types of monkeys in attendance, circled around the enclosure like it was an arena.

Clyde, Yohann and Taddy were crouching - looking from above, down into the enclosure.

"I can't see Diego," Clyde stated as he glanced around.

"I told you, coming here was a complete waste of time," Yohann snorted.

"I could have sworn I saw them take him here," Taddy muttered to herself.

"Take him?!" Clyde asked. "You never mentioned anything about him being taken?" he added.

"Oh yeah, he was taken," Taddy smiled awkwardly.

"So you're saying these apes took him?" Clyde asked.

"Well, yeah!" replied Taddy.

"She's making it up as she goes along," Yohann muttered.

As Clyde continued to glance around the ape enclosure he noticed some familiar faces.

"Is that Pierce and Preston?" he pointed out to Yohann. "Wait, they've got Nayha!" He added in horror.

Yohann and Taddy looked to where Clyde was pointing.

"Is that a squirrel?" Yohann asked, confused.

It appeared Nayha, Pierce, Preston and Nutz were being held captive; they were tied up but seemed to have score cards alongside them. It looked like they were being forced to be judges. The apes were continuing to cheer as the baboon MC carried on addressing them.

"We've got some incredibly talented acts for you this evening – our judges are certainly in for a treat. But without any further ado let's bring out the reason this amazing competition is happening in the first place, the reason why we are all here tonight. Make some noise for the zoo's biggest attraction – the one, the only, the almighty, the all-powerful KING IWATO!" The presenter announced as the crowd went wild.

As the baboon concluded his introduction, the ground of the zoo enclosure began to shake as a humongous gorilla walked out into the centre. The giant silverback was known as one of the biggest gorillas in the world. His long arms had enormous strength, his eyes would pierce through you if you looked up at his unkind face.

All of the different types of primates in the enclosure roared in delight as King Iwato acknowledged them and sat down upon his huge throne that was made up for him right alongside the new 'penguin judges'.

"What are they even doing here?" Clyde muttered as he looked down at his friends. "I bet they came looking for us," he added with a sigh.

"Oh well. No one asked them to – their funeral," Yohann shrugged.

"You don't really mean that!" responded Clyde.

"Well what can we do?" Yohann pointed out. "There's dozens of apes down there and only three of us!"

"Oh! I've just had an apostrophe!" Taddy gleamed with excitement.

"I think you mean an epiphany," Yohann replied bluntly.

"I feel as if lightning has just struck my brain!" Taddy added.

"That must have hurt," Yohann snorted.

"Honestly, guys, I think I actually have a really, really good idea!" Taddy insisted.

"It won't work." Yohann interrupted before giving Taddy the chance to explain.

"If you've got any decent suggestions, Yohann, I'd like to hear them!" Clyde said firmly to Yohann, causing him to back down. Clyde then turned his attention back to Taddy.

"Now this plan of yours," Clyde said with interest. "What is it?"

- X -

On the other side of the primates' enclosure Benjamin and his cronies were hidden on top of a roof of outdoor toilets that the pipe had led them to, dripping and stinking of sewage. Benjamin had pulled out a telescope and was peering at the apes, who were going wild.

"What's going on down there?" Denzel asked.

"I have absolutely no idea," Benjamin replied, puzzled as he continued to look down at the primates performing. "I've never seen anything like it. But," he added excitedly as his scope swiveled towards a penguin that unmistakably had a mohawk, "unless I'm very much mistaken I see our penguin down there."

"But how are we going to be able to get in there without bringing any suspicion to ourselves?" asked Norris.

Benjamin and Denzel both looked at each other before turning their attentions back to Norris.

"What?" Norris asked nervously.

FOURTEEN

Back in the ape enclosure Nayha, Pierce and Preston and the newly named squirrel 'Nutz' were tied up and being forced to judge the primate talent show.

"We need to get out of here," Nayha muttered to the others as she tried to break free.

"Really? I can think of worse things than being tied up to watch a talent show. I mean, you know why they took us, don't you?" Preston said to the others, causing them all to shrug their shoulders.

"Evidently my reputation in the industry of spotting talent is golden. These apes just want my stamp of approval. They should have just asked. This whole prisoner thing was completely unnecessary," explained Preston.

Even Nutz rolled his eyes at Preston's explanation.

"We need to go and find the others! Don't you get that Preston? We've gone from coming to save the others to needing to be saved ourselves!" Nayha said firmly.

"Look, everything will be fine! Just relax and enjoy the show!" Preston reassured.

The baboon presenter, Bob Boonhouse, took his spot back in the centre of the enclosure.

"It's time for our first contestant of the evening! It's the hilarious Mo the Monkey! The clown that makes us all go bananas!" The MC called out causing a cheer from the audience. A spider monkey dressed in a clown costume took centre stage; a bright orange wig, a red nose, white make up and a red long tailcoat with a black top hat. He wore polka dot trousers and big red shoes. He had a briefcase that he put down next to him.

Preston started to lose colour in himself and began to sweat and feel dizzy.

"Pierce," he whispered softly.

"What is it now?" Pierce muttered in frustration.

"I've never told anyone this, but I have coulrophobia," Preston stated.

"Coulrophobia? What's that?" Pierce asked, confused.

“It’s an extreme fear of clowns!” Preston said sternly. “I think I’m going to pass out,” he panted.

Pierce rolled his eyes before looking back at Preston who had slumped to the floor.

“Oh, he’s actually passed out,” Pierce said to himself in shock, before trying to get Nayha’s attention. “Nayha, I think Pierce has passed out. He’s scared of clowns,” Pierce whispered.

"Well, take it as a positive. It gives us some peace for a few minutes," said Nayha.

"Nayha?!" Pierce said in horror. "Don't you care about his discomfort?"

"Of course, but about an hour ago Preston heard one of those chimps use the word 'evidently' and he's used it about twelve times since. You're honestly telling me you wouldn't enjoy a Preston break?" Nayha explained.

Pierce looked at Nutz who simply shrugged his shoulders. "Fair point," Pierce muttered.

After the clown act had finished, Preston slowly came around and was able to watch the other acts that performed. One included a break-dancing chimp named 'Pirlo', who although looked the part with his sparkling jacket, bushy Afro and shades, didn't impress with his dance moves at all.

"EVIDENTLY, he hasn't been rehearsing as much as he's been taking care of that ghettolicious afro," Preston muttered to Pierce.

"I don't suppose we have anymore clowns?" Pierce called out to Bob Boonhouse.

Luckily for Preston there weren't any more clowns at the ready. Some of the other acts included:

A chimpanzee that could turn his hands around at 360 degree angles many times to the Mission Impossible soundtrack.

A small macaque monkey that could make his eyes vibrate.

Another chimp that could solve a Rubix cube in twelve seconds.

Many apes that had multiple tribute acts to the band 'Queen'.

"Pierce, we need to call for a break," Preston begged. "If I have to listen to 'We are the Champions' one more time I will scream!"

Pierce rolled his eyes and said, "Oh come on, it's not that ba…".

"I WILL SCREAM!" Preston interrupted.

"Will you guys calm down! We've just got one more to see. Then hopefully this madness will come to an end," Nayha said.

Bob Boonhouse came back to the centre of the enclosure again. "Ladies and Gents, we're very excited to announce our last act. The orangutan that's got the whole zoo talking… it's Miles!" A loud cheer erupted around the ape enclosure. "Trust me, ladies and gentlemen, Miles is going places," the presenter added.

"Well with a name like Miles, he's bound to," Preston muttered sarcastically to Pierce.

Miles entered the enclosure, took out a harmonica, seemingly to help him get in tune for something, before bizarrely laying down on the ground with his legs and bum in the air. To the penguins absolute horror he then proceeded to fart really loudly.

"What in the world?" Nayha muttered.

"This is a talent?!" Pierce whispered disapprovingly.

Nutz proceeded immediately by covering his nose. Farts from orangutans were an awful lot for a squirrel to handle.

"Well I admire him," Preston stated. "I know you guys wouldn't understand but this is very avant-garde… wait a minute, is that a tune I'm hearing?" Preston asked as he and the other penguins began to listen closely.

"Oh yeah, it's…" Nayha said before being immediately cut off by Preston.

"It's 'We are the Champions'! Stop this madness!" Preston screamed.

FIFTEEN

After Miles had finished his wonderful farting rendition of 'We are the Champions', it was time for a break before the judges had to announce the winner, although Miles the farting orangutan was certainly the red-hot favourite to win in the eyes of all of the primates in attendance.

"Before the judges announce the winner of tonight's incredible talent show, we have a very special act. Purely in honour of our incredible King Iwato, please welcome the amazing, the super talented, legendary, astonishing DIEGO the sensational penguin!"

Nayha, Preston and Pierce all gasped simultaneously, whereas Nutz wasn't really sure what was going on.

Diego made his way to the centre of the enclosure where he was prompted to bow before the humongous King Iwato, who nodded his approval back at Diego. It was clear Diego was also being held against his will as he had a rope tied around his neck with a sinister-looking ape holding onto the other end of it.

Diego glanced at the other penguins with a perplexed look on his face as to why they were there. But he also looked as if he was under strict instructions not to speak or act out of turn.

Music started playing around the enclosure. The song 'Don't Stop Believing' started to play out as the sinister-looking ape released Diego from his rope. That was when Diego's performance started. The whole enclosure gasped, cheered and applauded as throughout the song Diego performed many different jaw-dropping stunts and acrobatics for the audience – he even leapt through a ring of fire.

Diego got a standing ovation from the entire enclosure; even King Iwato stood and applauded in appreciation. But before Diego could even complete his bow, the sinister looking ape lassoed the rope around his neck and started to drag him back towards the rear of the ape enclosure.

But, just as this was happening, Bob Boonhouse, the MC for the evening, stepped forward looking a bit anxious as he addressed the rest of the enclosure. "Ladies and gentlemen – I have an announcement to make. Although this is very much against PGT procedure and regulations, it appears we have a final contestant that wishes to enter at the last minute."

The controversy of this announcement caused gasps and a stir around the enclosure – voices muttered and echoed all around. Even the sinister-looking ape that was guarding Diego couldn't help but shed a gasp.

There was an unsettled angst amongst the entire enclosure and King Iwato didn't like this, not one bit.

"SILENCE!" he yelled. His roar was like a strong wind gusting at you. The entire enclosure went silent as King Iwato addressed them.

"What is the meaning of this?" he asked aggressively. "PGT has been a successful, organised show for seven years now. Never have we allowed new applications this late into proceedings. How dare this ape try and bypass my ruling! Bring them to me so I can finish them!" He roared which caused a cheer from the primates.

"Looks like this show just got good," Pierce muttered to Preston.

The presenter, Bob Boonhouse, looked more and more anxious by the second. He was sweating buckets as he looked at a small card that he had received.

"With all due respect, Your Highness, this ape has travelled a great distance just so they can perform in front of you. He has come highly recommended from Prince Joe King from the zoo on the island of Goo - li - bal!" Bob explained as he read the card. "The act in question is a fantastic wizard."

This caused a little buzz of excitement from the apes in the enclosure. Although none of them had ever heard of that place.

"I've been there," Preston whispered to Nayha, which caused her to shake her head at him in response.

King Iwato looked deep in thought. He certainly didn't like the idea of changing the rules but he was intrigued by what this apparent act could do; however, he didn't want to appear weak to the other apes by changing his mind. An idea struck him before announcing:

"Very well... but if this wizard fails to impress me. I will crush him!" He roared as all the apes in the enclosure applauded and cheered.

"Okay," the presenter sighed in relief, before introducing the act.

"May I introduce to you, the magnificent wizard, the one, the only, 'THE GREAT

SPLENDINI'" he announced as a very strange looking ape entered the centre of the enclosure.

As Clyde and Yohann watched from above, they crossed their flippers. It was in fact just Taddy the cat, trying really hard to walk like an ape, and wearing a very strange robe.

King Iwato looked hard at Taddy's disguise. He clearly suspected something wasn't right. He sat down on his throne and grunted at her to get on with it.

"I have travelled from very, very far to be with you today, so that I could attend this prestigious event this evening. I have performed in front of lots of royalty but none had the wonderful reputation of performing here at the PGT competition in front of the mighty King Iwato," Taddy said, improvising most of what she was saying. But it seemed to be working. King Iwato seemed more relaxed and nodded his head in approval for the act to continue.

"Before I perform my first trick, for the magic powers to enter me, I need you all to be in deep meditation with me and allow the magic in me to fill up. So I ask you all to close your eyes and peacefully count with me down from twenty before the powerful magic and wonders are seen tonight." Taddy nervously explained, hoping the primates in the enclosure would buy it.

A lot of the primates looked at each other and at the king, not sure what to make of the request. King Iwato took a huge sigh – all of the primates now were focussed on him, looking at him for guidance. Thankfully King Iwato began to slowly close his eyes and the rest of the primates soon followed. Even Diego, Nayha, Preston, Pierce and Nutz all had their eyes closed.

"I shall begin," Taddy, in disguise as The Great Splendini, announced.

"Twenty!" she called out, but as she did, she began to beckon Clyde and Yohann, who had slowly started to climb their way down into the enclosure. They had to be so quiet – the slightest noise that raised any suspicion would cause BIG, BIG problems.

"Nineteen," Taddy called out as Clyde and Yohann slowly made their way over to the other penguins. Clyde headed for Diego, and Yohann went to the others.

"Eighteen, seventeen," Taddy called out, trying to create as much time as possible without causing any suspicion.

As Yohann untied Preston he quickly gagged his mouth with the rope knowing Preston would most likely give a huge over the top reaction to being saved, which would certainly disturb the apes.

"Sixteen... fifteen," Taddy continued, as Clyde slowly unhooked the rope from around the neck of Diego. Diego actually seemed very glad to see him, to Clyde's amazement.

"Fourteen... thirteen," said Taddy, as Clyde signalled for Diego to be quiet as they began to slowly creep away from the sinister looking baboon that was guarding Diego.

"Twelve... eleven... ten," Taddy nervously continued as she slowly began to creep away herself. "Nine, eight," she added.

Yohann had just finished releasing Nayha, Pierce and Preston and reluctantly Nutz - who he had no knowledge of - and they all began to creep out themselves.

"Seven... six," Taddy added, as Clyde and Diego had got some distance between themselves and the sinister-looking baboon.

Taddy got herself out of the enclosure - along with Yohann, Nayha, Pierce, Preston and Nutz. Clyde and Diego were so close!

Just as the escape was looking promising, a strange-looking figure started to appear in the distance. The figure seemed to have bits of hay, straw and litter stuck to him to try and make him look ape-like. He had soda cans for ears and a banana peel on top of his head. The figure also smelt really, really bad.

The penguins, Nutz and Taddy looked at the figure in complete confusion.

"What's he supposed to be?" Preston whispered to Pierce.

Unbeknownst to the penguins, the unconvincing-looking ape was Norris who was slowly making his way towards the penguins.

Benjamin and Denzel were quite far-off behind him - Benjamin had a walkie-talkie that he was instructing Norris on.

"Nice and slowly, Norris. Take your time, just make sure you get that penguin! Know that me and Denzel are right behind you," Benjamin said to him.

"Yeah, about 100 yards behind me," Norris snorted.

Norris's distraction had caught Taddy off-guard, who had accidentally stopped counting backwards, causing King Iwato to open one of his eyes; as soon as he realised there was no magical act about to appear and he'd been hoodwinked by these escapees, chaos struck. A roar of anger, such as you have never heard in your life, burst out of him.

"Mission abort!!!" Norris cried out as he started to sprint out of the enclosure towards Benjamin and Denzel. Luckily for Norris, the King was completely focused on the penguin group.

King Iwato leapt down from his throne and onto the ground, making it feel like a small earthquake had hit. More apes fell over, as did Clyde who was just about to climb out of the enclosure himself. Instead, he fell backwards. King Iwato was heading straight for him with tremendous speed. It looked like Clyde was just a few seconds away from being crushed as King Iwato jumped high into the air with his enormous, giant-like feet aiming towards Clyde.

Clyde knew he was only a few seconds away from becoming as flat as a pancake. He closed his eyes, hoping it would be painless. But the next thing he knew, with a lightning-bolt 'whooosh', someone grabbed him. Clyde opened his eyes and saw he was on Taddy's back along with Diego, who had come to Clyde's aid and grabbed him from the clutches of his horrible fate.

"You saved me!" called out Clyde.

"We're not out of the woods yet, amigo!" Diego replied as Taddy was dodging numerous other primates that were trying to grab them, while balancing both Clyde and Diego on her back. Nayha and the others watched in anxious horror.

"Please Clyde, next time I'm asleep, do me a favour – DON'T WAKE ME UP!" Taddy yelled, as King Iwato took another enormous leap in the air, hoping to crash down on them. He only missed by inches.

All these leaps were causing shakes round the entire enclosure. As Taddy continued to dart around, Clyde noticed a plank of wood that had fallen down on top of a small water barrel.

"I have a plan!" Clyde called out. "Head for the plank!" he added as Taddy followed his instructions and stood by the end of one of the planks.

"What are you doing?" asked Diego.

"Improvising!" replied Clyde.

"Well, now what?"

"Stay VERY, VERY still," Clyde instructed.

"WHAT?!?!" Taddy shrieked.

"That's suicide!" Diego added.

"Trust me, Taddy, don't move until I say so – got it?" said Clyde.

"I'll try!" Taddy replied nervously, "but when an eight hundred pound gorilla comes plummeting towards you, your first thought is to run! But fine, we'll do it your way – shall we kiss our butts goodbye now?!" Taddy added with a cry.

King Iwato once again jumped high into the air, descending closer and closer towards the three of them.

"This is madness!" Diego yelled.

"Can I move now!" screamed Taddy.

"Hold it… it needs to be just at the right moment," Clyde muttered nervously.

The huge feet of King Iwato had almost completely covered the three of them in darkness.

"Quick now! Other side of the plank!" Clyde cried as Taddy darted to the other side – she had never moved so quickly. Just as the three of them got to the other side of the plank, King Iwato landed on the now elevating original side – causing the three of them to be catapulted high up into the sky.

"AHHHHHHHHHHHH" they all screamed

as they rose high above the enclosure, looking down at the other penguins and Nutz gasping up at them.

Clyde was trying to remain as focussed as he could as they ascended.

"Diego, we could really use your sky diving experience in teaching us how to land safe right about now," Clyde called out to him.

Diego started to look very worried and reluctant to answer.

"Like right now please!" Clyde shouted.

"About that..." Diego replied anxiously as

the three of them stopped rising and were about to begin their drop down into the zoo.

"What?" Clyde asked with concern.

"It's been so long, I'm not really sure I remember any of my training," Diego called out.

"Well that's just super!" Clyde yelled out sarcastically. "This part of my plan was kind of banking on you remembering," he added, before looking down at his zoo surroundings. "What do we do now?!" He cried out with a loss of hope. The three of them were beginning to fall down FAST!

"Aim for the tent!" Taddy yelled as she pointed out a large tent next to the ape enclosure where different kids' shows were performed during the day for families. They all headed for it, hoping for the best landing possible. As they hit the tent they all broke straight through it and landed in boxes filled with goodie bag items.

"Are we alive?" Clyde whispered.

"Either that or heaven has got a weird sense of humour," Diego replied after looking at the bunch of soft toy monkeys he had landed in, all repeating the words "I love you" to him in unison.

"Pretty sure I'm down to the last three of my nine lives now," Taddy added as she crawled out of a box of hand puppets.

The other penguins and Nutz had all rushed into the tent after witnessing the dramatic fall.

"Thank the stars you're all okay!" said Nayha.

"Just to clarify, are you a real wizard or not?" Preston asked Taddy, which resulted in a lot of stern eyes looking at him.

"Evidently not," he muttered to himself.

SIXTEEN

"Is everyone okay?" Pierce called out.

"Somehow!" Clyde replied.

"Lucky, lucky, lucky us! I can't believe we're all in one piece," Taddy muttered in shock.

"Guys this is Taddy, she was so important in helping us tonight. We couldn't have done it without her," Clyde said as he introduced her.

"You're a cat?" Preston called out.

"Yes!" Taddy replied excitedly.

"You know what they are?" Pierce said confused. "Have you seen one before?" he asked.

"Only from Andrew Lloyd Webber's masterpiece," Pierce answered.

"And who's this little guy?" Clyde asked as he approached Nutz.

"This is our little squirrel friend who helped us out today," Pierce answered.

"We named him Nutz," Preston added. "He's our new honorary penguin," he said before turning his attention to Pierce.

"I was thinking Pierce, why don't we keep him with us? He can come back with us and we can take care of him? I mean, he's vulnerable out there all on his own. Surely he deserves a family?" Preston nervously asked.

Pierce took a look at Nutz who seemed to like the idea. He looked back at Pierce, smiling. Pierce turned his attention back to Clyde.

"What do you think Clyde?" he asked.

"Well if it's what you guys would like, and if Nutz is happy to adapt to a penguin lifestyle and be with us all then I can't think of two better penguins to care for him as much as you two," Clyde answered.

Preston and Pierce smiled with glee before giving their adopted squirrel 'Nutz' a huge hug.

Clyde looked at Taddy.

"How about you? Do you fancy moving in?" Clyde asked.

Taddy smiled at him but politely turned down his request. "It's a lovely offer. But I like to roam around far too much. But I will certainly be visiting you all an awful lot, if that's okay?" she said.

"That's more than okay," Clyde replied.

"Well if you'll all excuse me. I'm going to find somewhere I can get some shut eye. It's awfully late. Farewell all," Taddy said, as she skipped away out of the tent.

Clyde looked towards Yohann. "Are you crying?" Clyde asked in shock.

"It's just allergies," Yohann snorted back. "The material of the tent is clearly making my eyes water," he explained.

"Sure," Clyde replied sarcastically.

Nayha approached Clyde. "I'm so glad you're okay. I'm sorry I was angry at you. I just didn't get why you did something so stupid," she explained.

"It was just jealousy, I suppose." Clyde answered. "I almost felt like I was being replaced and I guess it hurt me seeing you fall for Diego… I'm so sorry Nayha."

"Fall for him?" Nayha asked, confused. "You stupid fool, Clyde. I wasn't falling for Diego. Sure, I was impressed by him and it was kind of cool learning all about his background. It was just exciting for everyone. There's only one penguin I've always been falling for. I just wish he'd open his eyes and see that," Nayha explained before kissing Clyde on the cheek and slowly walking away.

Clyde began to blush. His feathers began to quiver because of the goose bumps he felt. "Let's go home," he sighed to himself.

As he and the penguins all began to waddle out of the tent, Clyde noticed that Diego was behind them and not following them.

"Come on Diego – lets go home!" Clyde called out to him.

"I'm not coming, amigo," Diego called back, which caused a stir amongst the other penguins.

"What?!" Clyde asked, as he started to approach Diego. "Why?" he added.

"I will not be a prisoner any longer!" Diego yelled.

Clyde started to feel his blood boil; he had risked his life and the lives of others to try and save Diego and bring him back, but now he wasn't coming home.

"You guys head back to Penguin Beach… we'll catch up," Clyde called out to the others as he came face to face with Diego.

"We are NOT going without you," Nayha called back sternly.

"Yohann, guys, please just get everyone back to the Beach safely. We'll be right there," Clyde instructed.

Pierce approached Nayha. "Come on Nayha – let them do what they gotta do. They won't be far behind us," he said as he ushered her out of the tent with the others.

"Don't waste your time, amigo. I'm not going with you," Diego stated.

"Waste my time? How about me and everybody else not only wasting our time but RISKING OUR LIVES to bring you back?" Clyde shouted.

"I didn't ask them to," Diego shrugged.

"I thought you'd perhaps be a little more grateful for having your life saved! But no, your ego only ever cares about yourself!" replied Clyde.

"Saving my life? No, amigo, I think you'll find it was me that saved your life. If it wasn't

for me, you'd be getting scraped off a gorilla's foot by monkey butlers right now!" Diego stated, getting more and more angry himself.

"I was there to save you!" Clyde screamed in frustration.

"Well, I guess that makes us even! Anyway, you've certainly changed your tune. What happened to encouraging me to be free?" he asked.

"I WAS TRYING TO GET RID OF YOU!" Clyde yelled.

Diego was taken aback by this, before beginning to grin to himself.

"Now it all makes sense. Well, amigo, why don't you let me go ahead and get rid of myself from YOUR penguin kingdom?" He responded before starting to walk away.

"Look, Diego," Clyde sighed, "I made a mistake. I never should have encouraged you to leave. Please stay. I want you to. You have friends here."

"I don't do friends." Diego muttered to himself.

"You have penguins that care about you. You can be part of a family," Clyde pleaded.

"Family? Let me tell you something about family. I was ripped away from my family when I was a child. Forced to perform. I've been dragged from circus to circus, stage to stage. There's no such thing as families, all they do is hold you back, drag you down and break your heart," Diego muttered sincerely.

"What's going on, Diego? What on earth is running away going to achieve? You've still managed to have all those amazing adventures that any other penguin could only dream about. Don't you get lonely? Sure, you can go sky diving, relax on the beach and go on all the different adventures you want but isn't having friends the ultimate adventure?" Clyde asked.

"But that's it! I've never really done any of those things!" Diego snapped as he turned around to face Clyde.

"What do you mean?" Clyde asked, confused.

"I LIED!" Diego yelled. "I've never done any of those things. I've been a prisoner my ENTIRE LIFE. As long as I remember I've been trained to jump, dance, jump through hoops and perform tricks for audiences across the world. I've NEVER been free," Diego explained.

"Why did you lie?" asked Clyde.

"It wasn't to hurt you. I'm sorry if it did. I've never had friends or a family. All I've ever had is a trainer and an audience. I guess I just lied about having done all these exciting things and living this amazing lifestyle so you would all find me interesting, want to be my friend, think I was worth having around, not as a performer but just as a fellow penguin! I wasn't lying to belittle or make you feel bad. Maybe it wasn't even about impressing everyone – I guess maybe I was just lying because I wanted to be loved," Diego explained.

The anger from Clyde slowly melted away. He felt for the first time that he really understood Diego.

"And you can be loved Diego. But you need to stay here with friends," Clyde explained once more.

"I don't do friends… it never works out and I won't be a prisoner anymore," Diego stated before slowly walking away from the tent.

"Diego!" Clyde called out in a desperate attempt to stop him.

But Diego had gone.

SEVENTEEN

Diego continued to walk around the zoo, searching for the easiest way to break free. Something inside him did want to turn around but he couldn't – not now he'd confessed to Clyde the truth about himself.

'How would they ever accept me now?' he thought sadly.

"There must be a way to break out of here somewhere…" Diego muttered, as he ventured along different paths around the zoo, hoping to find an opening he could escape from. As he became more anxious about finding a way out he noticed a huge poster of himself that advertised him as 'Diego the Incredible'.

Diego looked at the poster of himself and felt a complete fraud. 'Incredible' was the last thing he felt.

"Gee, and I thought I was vain," a voice said towards Diego's right. Diego looked and saw a group of lemurs staring at him.

The same voice continued to speak. It was the lemur at the front of the group. "Sorry, but I have to ask, what are you doing out there?" the lemur queried, as he and the other lemurs seemed baffled to see a penguin free to roam around the zoo.

"Who are you?" Diego asked cautiously. He didn't want a similar experience to the one he had with the apes.

"Of course! Where are my manners?" the lemur chuckled. "Allow me to introduce myself – my name is Liam!" He smiled.

"Your name is Liam?" Diego asked.

"Correct!" Liam answered.

"Your name is Liam… the lemur," Diego replied slowly.

"I know – original right?!" Liam chuckled. "Anyway, back to my point. What are you doing out there?"

"I'm escaping. I'm breaking free from this zoo," Diego explained, causing a gasp from the other lemurs.

"Escape from the zoo? But why?" Liam asked, very puzzled.

"Don't you ever think about breaking out of that cage and being free? Who wants to be a prisoner?" Diego explained.

"A prisoner?!" Liam jumped in shock as all the other Lemurs gasped. Liam turned his attention to the rest of lemurs.

"I think I'm going to have to sing the song," Liam muttered to them.

"Oh no… not the song," one gloomy-looking lemur moaned.

Liam turned his attention back to Diego.

"My penguin friend, let me explain something to you," said Liam as he prepared to burst out in song:

"There's a place where the big, bright moon
Makes the monkeys swing
And the lions swoon
Where the zebras nap when they have the chance
And us lemurs, hey we like to sing and dance!
All the animals are intertwined
As we get on with our day

It's the zoo life!
Plenty for all to eat
The people come
To have some fun
And we get to meet and greet
It's the zoo life!
Keeping those predators at bay!
Being free more like a family
Is what the zoo can bring!"

Liam sang as the other lemurs joined in every so often and danced to Liam's catchy song.

Diego couldn't help but look at all the lemurs together and feel their sense of family; something that he longed to feel for himself. He realised he could have had that with the other penguins.

"You need to stop seeing a prison! Sure, it may be hard work sometimes! But is it worth it to be safe, have a home and family? Of course!" said Liam.

Diego couldn't help but smile. "You're completely right, amigo … I will get back to Penguin Beach right away!" he said as he started to rush away.

"Good luck to you, my friend! Haha!" Liam called out to Diego.

Diego started to hurry back as quickly as he could – he knew in his heart that the other penguins would certainly accept him back. For the first time in Diego's life he felt like he could have a family.

He rushed past many different animals to find his way back to Penguin Beach. But as he ran he came to a sudden stop.

He froze as he looked up and saw three humans staring down at him.

It was Benjamin Blacker with his associates, Denzel and Norris.

"I don't believe it! It's almost too good to be true," Benjamin gasped.

"Surely that can't be the penguin we want?" Denzel asked. "It's too easy," he added.

"Yeah, I mean, shouldn't it be in a cage or something?" Norris added.

"Oh it's him!" Benjamin assured them both. "Call it destiny," he began to chuckle to himself. "Get him," he ordered as Denzel smothered Diego into a huge sack. Diego tried his best to put up as much of a fight as he could to try and escape but what with Norris' big fat body jumping on the sack, while Denzel tied it together, there wasn't anything Diego could do.

Watching this all unfold was Taddy, who had been trying to sleep nearby. "I've got to tell the others!" she gasped to herself, before sprinting off to inform the other penguins.

EIGHTEEN

"Would you like your face painted like a pretty pink butterfly tomorrow?" Pierce asked as he looked affectionately down at Nutz.

"No, I'm just not in the mood," Preston sighed before Pierce gave him a sarcastic look. "Oh, of course…" Preston muttered, rather embarrassed, after realising that Pierce was in fact talking to Nutz and not him.

As the penguins approached Penguin Beach, Clyde caught up with them.

"No Diego?" Nayha asked as Clyde approached her.

"He's made his choice," Clyde replied rather sternly, feeling both sadness and anger that Diego had decided to leave them.

"Maybe it's for the best," Nayha sighed, "if it's what will make him happiest."

As they made their way back, they were greeted by Anton who was the first to notice them.

"I'm Anton! I'm Anton!" he yelled and pointed to them, which alerted the others.

"You're back!" said Pam, overjoyed, as she and Bobby approached them.

"We were so worr…" Bobby began.

"We were so worried!" interrupted Pam.

Arthur slowly began to waddle out of the cave, making sure all the penguins had returned safely.

"No Diego?" He asked Clyde.

Clyde looked down disappointedly. "No, Arthur, and I'm sorry," Clyde replied.

"Do we know if he's alive?" Arthur asked.

"He is," Clyde answered.

"We found him and he's safe now. Clyde told him to come back but he wouldn't listen. He really did just want to go," explained Nayha.

"Is that true?" asked Arthur.

"It is," replied Clyde.

"Clyde, you're a good penguin. But sometimes even good penguins can do bad things… stupid things. I just hope you've learnt from this?" Arthur asked.

"I have," Clyde assured him.

Arthur looked at Nutz, rather confused. "After such a long day, I think I'll pass for now," he said, fighting the urge to question just what a squirrel was doing in Penguin Beach.

"PENGUINS! PENGUINS!" a voice yelled from outside Penguin Beach.

"What's that?" Arthur quizzed as the voice echoed again, "PENGUINS! PENGUINS!"

"Taddy?" Clyde muttered to himself. "Taddy, is that you?"

Taddy leapt up on to the wall that surrounded Penguin Beach.

"You've got to come quick! It's Diego! I think he's being birdnapped!" Taddy said in a panic.

All the penguins looked at each other with worry - even Yohann showed concern.

"Birdnapped? What do you mean birdnapped?" asked Clyde.

"Three scary-looking men grabbed him and put him in a sack! I think they're taking him away somewhere!" Taddy explained.

Clyde didn't say anything; he just looked at the ground deep in thought.

"Well?!" Taddy yelled, "don't just stand there - let's go and save him!"

Clyde continued to not respond.

"Clyde?" Nayha asked gently.

Clyde turned around and looked at Nayha then back to Taddy. "Well he wanted an adventure, didn't he? Looks like he finally got one," Clyde stated, before turning around and heading for the cave.

"Ouch," Preston muttered to Pierce.

"You can't just walk away!" Taddy yelled at him. "He needs your help."

Clyde turned his attention back to Taddy.

"I already tried saving him, remember? What happened? He turned around and took our kindness and threw it back in our face. He's on his own," Clyde explained.

"You're going to help him," Nayha said sternly. "Listen Clyde, I know you're upset and angry with Diego right now. But it's like Arthur said, you're a good penguin and I know that you won't leave Diego when he needs you." Nayha said.

Clyde sighed. He knew she was right.

"Then we'd better hurry. I'm coming, Taddy. Wait right there!" Clyde called out to her.

"Show us the way," Yohann added.

Clyde seemed shocked and taken aback by what Yohann had said.

"Listen Yohann, I appreciate it but I can't ask you to come with me," Clyde said before addressing all the other penguins.

"That goes for all of you. I've put you guys through too much already. Some of you have risked your lives because of me. You can't do that again."

Preston approached Clyde with a serious look on his face.

"Clyde, when will you get it? We are penguins! We waddle together, we peck together and we fight together! We're doing this TOGETHER! As a family."

"All of us," Nayha added with a smile.

Clyde looked proudly at all the penguins around him, as well as Nutz and Taddy. He finally looked at Arthur who simply nodded his head at him.

"Let's do this!"

Clyde grinned.

NINETEEN

Benjamin, Denzel and Norris were desperately trying to stop Diego from fighting his way out of the sack so they could make their way back out of the zoo. They headed towards the toilets, their original point of entry.

"Something smells REALLY bad," Norris said aloud.

"It's you," Denzel replied bluntly.

"Me?! I was being polite! It's you!" Norris yelled.

"It's all of us!" Benjamin snapped at them. "It's from that dirty sewer and climbing through all those drains! I dread to think of the human and animal excrement we've pushed our way through."

As Benjamin said this, laughter was heard and an aggressive cackling sound pierced through them. They turned and realised they were next to the hyena cage and were facing Snicker and Heckle who were in hysterics.

"Oh shut up!" Benjamin yelled at them, which only caused the two hyenas to laugh even more.

"Are they laughing at us?" Norris asked.

"They're laughing at you," Denzel muttered.

"It's not me that stinks! It's you!" Norris snapped back at him.

"Oh stop it, you two!" Benjamin said to them sternly, as the two hyenas laughed louder and louder. "They're hyenas. They laugh at everything. They're pathetic animals. Very dumb. I mean look at them they're... wait... is that a joke book?" Benjamin said, confused, as he looked down at the hyenas' legs.

As Benjamin looked curiously at the two hyenas, something had caught the eyes of both Denzel and Norris.

"What on earth?" Denzel gasped.

"Uhhh...boss?" Norris muttered.

Benjamin turned his attention to what both Denzel and Norris were looking at and became just as bewildered as them.

"Another penguin?" he said, puzzled.

"Why are these penguins allowed to roam around the zoo?" Norris asked.

"They must have gotten loose," Denzel replied.

The penguin was Clyde and he was standing about forty yards away from them.

"Don't get nervous, Clyde," Clyde muttered to himself.

He looked over towards Preston, Pierce and Nutz, who had grabbed an old tape recorder that they kept in the cave for music. They also had a megaphone which they had grabbed from Penguin Beach that some of the staff used around the zoo. Nutz held down the button to

the megaphone and Pierce pressed the button on the tape recorder so the sound could be heard and echoed around them. Completely coincidently the song that was played from the tape recorder was 'We are the Champions' by Queen.

"Really?" Preston said to Pierce, very unimpressed.

Clyde heard the music and started to improvise his Irish dance moves to the song.

Benjamin, Denzel and Norris watched in pure confusion as Clyde danced.

"What's happening?" Norris muttered to the other two.

As Benjamin observed Clyde dance, he only saw the opportunity to make more money.

"I think we may have found ourselves another act…" Benjamin smirked.

Benjamin envisioned the extra money that would come rolling in from having Clyde in his grasp as well. Little did he notice the presence of the two other penguins.

Nayha and Yohann had slowly crept behind the three of them and began to tie their shoelaces together.

At the same time, Arthur and Ray had managed to sneak their way into the security office and after a few failed attempts to wake the zoo's elderly security guard, who was in a deep sleep, they managed to get hold of a phone and dial the police, trying to sound as unsuspicious as possible.

"Yes, you must get to the zoo at once! It appears there's a break-in currently underway. Make haste! My name? Erm… my name is…" Arthur panicked as his mind went blank and quickly looked around for something he could say. He noticed different posters of animals in the office, "Mr Jellyfish… yes, Mr Jellyfish… now, quickly!" Arthur said down the phone.

"If you could ask them to bring some warm cocoa, it would be very much appreciated," Ray asked.

Back in the zoo, Clyde continued to dance as Nayha and Yohann were slowly tying Denzel and Norris's shoelaces together. Once they had successfully done this, they carefully made their way to the feet of Benjamin.

"I want that penguin," Benjamin stated. "Bring him to me," he ordered, as he grabbed the sack that Diego was in from Norris.

"With pleasure," Denzel grinned.

"Right away," Norris said.

But as they stepped forward, they fell face first onto the ground. Nayha and Yohann hadn't had the chance to make a start on Benjamin's laces and had to make an almighty dive out of the way as Denzel and Norris hit the floor. As they lay there groaning in pain, the sound of sirens was heard echoing closer and closer to the zoo.

"The police!" Benjamin gasped before running away, laces still intact, attempting to get back to his escape route in time, leaving both Norris and Denzel lying on the ground.

Benjamin ran as fast as he could to get to the zoo toilets as quickly as possible but when he reached them he would encounter a problem: Bobby and Pam. As Benjamin went to open the toilet door, a big bucket of water fell directly on his head, pushed down on him by the penguin couple from the roof of the toilet block.

Benjamin fell over with the

bucket on his head and dropped the sack that Diego was in. Benjamin battled with the bucket stuck on his head for a while, as Bobby took a leap and made his way for the sack that Diego was wriggling around in.

Benjamin took the bucket off his head and looked up at the roof, seeing Pam looking down at him.

"YOU STUPID PENGUIN!" Benjamin screamed at her, throwing the bucket up at Pam, and catching her with it in the process.

Bobby saw this and it momentarily took his attention away from the sack Diego was in.

"Nobody talks to my wife like that, except for me!" Bobby yelled, launching himself towards Benjamin. "AWHHHHHH!"

He jumped on Benjamin, pecking at his face. There was a big struggle between Bobby and Benjamin before, finally, the penguin thief grabbed Bobby and threw him with force towards Pam, where he landed on the roof with quite a hard thud.

Benjamin could now hear the police cars directly outside the zoo. He knew they'd be making their way inside very shortly. He realised he needed somewhere to try and hide – and quick!

He grabbed the sack that Diego was in and quickly ran to find a hiding place.

Back on the roof, Bobby was a bit dazed and dizzy from his landing.

"Are you okay?" Pam asked, as she quickly rushed over towards her husband.

"I think so. Are you?" Bobby murmured.

"You're my hero!" Pam said, before beginning to smooch Bobby with lots of kisses.

Benjamin continued to run, desperately trying to find a hiding place or escape route of some kind. Little did he know he was being closed in on by another penguin; Clyde was riding on top of Taddy, chasing Benjamin and trying to save Diego.

Benjamin was sprinting towards a small building.

"HOLD ON TIGHT!" Taddy yelled to Clyde, as she lunged towards Benjamin – the opening from the door was getting smaller and smaller as Benjamin shut it.

Clyde closed his eyes. He was positive both him and Taddy were going to slam right into the door. But to his, and even Taddy's, surprise they had managed to make their way into the building by a whisker. Just in the nick of time.

And the building was the reptile house.

TWENTY

Benjamin hadn't noticed that both Clyde and Taddy had made their way into the reptile house with him. As soon as he shut the door, he slid all the locks across and looked through the small window on the door to see if he could see anyone coming.

'They're probably dealing with Denzel and Norris right now,' he muttered to himself, hoping it would bide him some time. He needed to come up with a plan.

Hidden in the dim light of the reptile house, Clyde and Taddy watched the thief, panting heavily.

"Got a plan?" Taddy muttered to Clyde.

"I guess I've just been improvising," Clyde replied anxiously.

"Got it!" Taddy replied with a smirk.

Clyde was slightly worried by the glee that had spread over her face.

"What are you doing?" Clyde asked, as Taddy locked her eyes onto Benjamin.

"Improvising!" Taddy replied as she started her sprint.

"Wait! Stop!" Clyde called out to her but it was too late. Taddy was leaping straight towards Benjamin.

She jumped into the air with her sharp claws drawn out, ready to land directly on Benjamin's head.

"OWWWAAAHAHAHAHAHA," Benjamin screamed as Taddy's long sharp claws dug into him. She hopped up and down on his head, digging her claws into him deeper and deeper with each leap. A struggle between Benjamin and Taddy broke out but with one final jump, Taddy scratched her claws across his face repeatedly.

Benjamin's screams echoed. "AWHAHAHA," he bellowed. It was so loud that even the police could hear a disturbance coming from the direction of the reptile house.

With that scream Benjamin had accidentally thrown the sack holding Diego on the floor.

It landed on a warm sandy surface.

Clyde looked on and gasped as he realised it was in the snake pit where Cuddles resided.

TWENTY-ONE

Clyde quickly dived into the snake pit and darted to the bag that Diego was in, hoping he would get to him in time before Cuddles the python sensed them both. Clyde couldn't help but notice the large stick that he and Yohann had used previously to get the better of Cuddles. He quickly untied the sack so Diego was free.

"Amigo!" Diego called out, embracing Clyde with a huge hug as he did so. "I'm so glad you found me!" Diego added.

"Diego, we can do this later but right now we really need to…" Clyde tried explaining before being cut off by Diego again.

"No, no. I need to say this now. Clyde, I was wrong about…" Diego tried to say, before being cut off.

"Diego we haven't got time! We need to leave right now!"

"I just need to say that..." Diego started.

"We are in grave danger here! We need to leave immediately!" Clyde cried.

"Danger? Why?" Diego asked, but as he said this he sensed a sinister presence behind him.

Clyde was staring directly at the red glaring eyes he had come across earlier that night. Cuddles was staring right at him.

"Because of that," Clyde sighed with worry as he pointed behind Diego.

Diego looked behind him. "Uh oh," he muttered as Cuddles the python leapt towards them. Clyde and Diego quickly darted out of the way, escaping the lunge from his jaws.

"Fancied your luck again, eh penguin? Didn't you learn to quit while you were ahead?" Cuddles hissed.

"It was just a flying visit!" Clyde sarcastically replied. "We'll be on our way now," he added, as he and Diego continued to try and escape the grasp of Cuddles, diving right and left to avoid his jaws.

Diego noticed a chance for them to escape. Diego was sure that if they were very quick, they could climb up the rockery to escape the pit.

"Clyde, now's our chance!" Diego yelled, as he jumped up towards the rockery. "Follow me!" he yelled.

As Diego started to climb, he looked back and noticed that Clyde wasn't following him. Clyde was still lying down in the pit after diving out of the way and Cuddles was starting to come back around, after being dazed by his landing.

"Clyde? What are you doing? Let's go!" Diego yelled.

Clyde reluctantly looked at Diego. "I'm hurt," he sighed, "I can't get up."

"What's wrong?" Diego called out worriedly.

"It's my leg. I can't stand up," Clyde explained.

"Clyde..." Diego said as his heart sank. He noticed that Cuddles was already beginning to eye up Clyde's position in the pit and preparing another lunge towards him.

"It's okay, Diego. You go. Leave me. Just tell everyone I'm so sorry... I'm sorry for everything," Clyde called out.

Diego faced the rocks he was climbing to escape, unsure what to do. He was just a few inches from freedom but the sight of Clyde's helpless body stopped him from going anywhere.

Clyde looked directly at Cuddles' eyes.

Cuddles began to laugh with a hissing tone.

"End of the line, bird," he said in an ominous voice.

"The offer's still there to hug it out." Clyde sarcastically replied.

Cuddles started an enormous lunge towards him, his jaws opened wide as it looked apparent Clyde was going to be swallowed whole.

There was a mighty crash as Cuddles landed on the ground towards Clyde. But as Cuddles came to, he was horrified to realise he hadn't devoured a penguin at all.

Diego had pushed Clyde out of the way without a second to spare.

"Are you mad?!" Clyde yelled at him.

"Maybe so," Diego replied, "But if we go down, we go down together. We're family."

They knew they only had a few seconds before Cuddles would come back to attack them both.

"I'm sorry you didn't get that adventure," Clyde said to Diego.

"Are you kidding, amigo?" replied Diego. "You've given me the best kind of adventure!" he smiled.

Before they could say anything else to each other, they saw Cuddles heading straight for them, his scaly face was filled with hatred, anger and rage.

But just as Cuddles got closer, another penguin leapt towards his back.

TWENTY-TWO

"I'm a tree!" The voice called out. The penguin in question seemed to be holding a stuffed toy penguin as he flew through the air and onto the back of Cuddles.

"That's Anton!" Clyde called out.

"Has he completely lost his mind?" Diego shrieked.

Cuddles was clearly very agitated and immediately turned his attention from Clyde and Diego onto Anton.

Diego dragged Clyde to the corner of the pit in a desperate attempt get Clyde to his feet.

Meanwhile Anton was riding on top of Cuddles like a pony, though it was more like being strapped to the back of a raging bull.

Diego was trying his hardest to get Clyde back onto his feet but to no avail.

"Why did you come back? You didn't have to. You would have been free," said Clyde.

"I had to come back. You would have done the same for me. It's what amigos do," replied Diego.

Cuddles had finally flung Anton off his back, throwing him against the rockery in the pit and leaving him unconscious on the ground, still clutching onto Gary. Cuddles once again turned his attention straight to Clyde and Diego. It looked like their luck had run out. There was no way Clyde was getting to his feet and there was less chance of Diego leaving Clyde alone.

"Now we end this," Cuddles hissed at them.

Diego hugged Clyde. "Gracias amigo, it's been emotional," he said, as Cuddles began to slither forward towards them deciding to slowly bide his time before pouncing on them.

"It really has," Clyde replied back to him.

But then, to their surprise, they suddenly saw Benjamin in the snake pit with Taddy in his grasp.

"Oh no, no, no, no, Mr Snake, you don't want to eat these penguins! They are far too yucky and horrible tasting to bother with," Benjamin started saying to the snake. He didn't want the snake to swallow them as, after all, they were far too valuable to him.

"You need to eat this ever so tasty, scrumptious cat. Trust me, it's much more appetising than a couple of lousy penguins," Benjamin negotiated with Cuddles.

Cuddles' head was ever so slightly turned towards Benjamin. Eating a whole cat certainly sounded very appealing to him. He slowly started to slither his way towards Benjamin, licking his lips at the prospect of feasting on Taddy.

Benjamin was waiting for the perfect moment to throw Taddy into the jaws of Cuddles. He needed enough time to grab his sack and take both Clyde and Diego.

"What do we do?" Clyde muttered to Diego.

Diego scanned the surroundings as fast as he could; there was no luck. He couldn't see anything he could use to help him. He then got up and waddled towards Cuddles and Benjamin, who was still holding Taddy aloft.

"Wait! What do you think you're doing?!" Clyde whispered to him frantically.

"Improvising," Diego said to him with a wink. "This could well be my final performance, amigo. It's been an honour," he said before running towards the situation.

"Diego, no!" Clyde called out.

Benjamin saw that Diego was heading towards himself and Cuddles and also started to panic.

"Get away from the snake, you stupid penguin! How will you perform if he eats you! What will I do then?!" Benjamin muttered.

But just as Benjamin uttered these words, that's exactly what Diego did – performed.

He started to perform his flips, tricks, jumps and dance moves around both Benjamin and Cuddles. This started to get Cuddles very, very irritated and he turned his focus back towards Diego.

Diego noticed this and prepared to dash away with his flippers entangling Bejamin's

legs as Cuddles followed him. Benjamin started to stumble with all the commotion going on around his legs.

Clyde noticed what Diego was trying to do.

"That's it, Diego! Keep going!" he shouted.

Benjamin was starting to lose his balance as he swayed back and forth, wobbling from the chase that was pursuing around, over and through his legs. Benjamin suddenly lost his balance and fell over face first into the sand of the pit, letting go of Taddy who landed on her feet.

"Quick Taddy, now!" Clyde yelled towards her as she dashed to Diego, who hopped onto her back to get away from both Cuddles and Benjamin.

As Benjamin came to his senses, he looked up and realised with horror he was face to face with a python. Cuddles hissed and licked his lips and before Benjamin could try to get back to his feet, he found himself in the jaws of Cuddles, slowly being swallowed whole.

Cuddles took his time as the body of one Benjamin Blacker began to sink lower and lower into the snake's body.

As this was going on, Taddy quickly put Clyde, Anton and Diego onto her back and climbed out of the rockery to escape from the pit.

The door to the reptile house burst open and police completely swarmed the entire building.

They soon noticed that their suspect was indeed inside the snake. Cuddles had almost instantly fallen asleep due to such a hefty snack.

"I've never seen anything like it," the inspector said to one of his officers.

"You have to give it to him – it's certainly a nifty hiding place," the officer replied.

"I suppose we better take that snake into custody. I think I'll let you get in the pit and see to that…" said the inspector.

The penguins and Taddy hid as they observed the officers slowly and carefully make their way into the pit to grab Cuddles.

"Another close escape," Taddy chuckled softly. "Where to next?" she added.

"Let's get back to Penguin Beach," Diego replied, smiling at both Clyde and Anton.

"I JUST RODE A UNICORN!" Anton said in delight.

TWENTY-THREE

Taddy was exhausted as she carried Clyde, Diego and Anton back to Penguin Beach where all the others were gathered waiting for their return.

"Thank the stars you are all back okay!" Nayha said in relief, as she rushed over to hug all the penguins and Taddy.

Anton hopped off the cat's back with excitement.

"I just rode a unicorn!" he shouted.

"I bet it wasn't a real unicorn," Preston muttered to Pierce.

Diego slowly got off Taddy's back and supported Clyde as he got off last. Clyde was still finding it hard to stand up after his battle with Cuddles in the snake pit.

"What happened?" Nayha asked.

"Long story," Diego said, "but we got through it together, didn't we Clyde?"

"We certainly did, amigo," Clyde smiled.

Bobby and Pam approached them all, hand in hand. "We're so glad you're all back safe," Bobby smiled.

"It's so nice that we are all back home together," Pam smiled as she looked lovingly into Bobby's eyes before the two slowly walked away, Bobby's flipper over Pam's shoulder.

"Did I hit my head harder than I thought in that pit? Or did that actually just happen?" Clyde asked.

"They've been like it since we've been back. It's like they've fallen in love all over again – it's adorable," Nayha smiled.

"Seeing it warms my heart," Ray smiled. For once he wasn't moaning about the cold.

"It's disgusting," Yohann grunted.

Arthur slowly made his way over to both Clyde and Diego.

"It's great to have you both back," Arthur smiled. "Diego, you're more than welcome here. I hope you know that. This can be your home – if you want it to be."

"If you'd be so kind as to welcome me here. I'd love to call this my home. I have friends here after all," said Diego.

"No, you don't," Clyde replied bluntly, which caused a look of confusion on everyone's faces.

"You have a family," Clyde smiled, before giving his new amigo Diego a hug and a pat on the back.

Pierce looked hard at Preston, convinced he was going to cry any second.

"I'm not going to cry… I'm not… I'm not. I won't!" Preston tried reassuring himself as he held back the tears, but to his and Pierce's surprise it was Yohann who started blubbering away.

"What? I'm not made of stone, you idiots!" Yohann said, as Pierce and Preston stared at him.

"Evidently not," replied Preston.

TWENTY-FOUR

As for Denzel Driscoll and Norris Bishop, they are now in prison. Their fellow inmates at the jail think they are both absolutely crazy due to the stories they tell them about being ambushed by a bunch of penguins.

Surgeons of the highest degree are currently examining Cuddles the snake in an obscure laboratory, trying to come up with a way they can remove Benjamin Blacker from the python's stomach. They are able to communicate with him daily by walkie-talkies after throwing one deep into Cuddles' stomach. Benjamin's mother comes in every night to use the walkie-talkie to tell him a bedtime story – whether Benjamin wants her to or not!

As for the penguins, life has never been so perfect for them at Penguin Beach. They all perform different acts together as a family and the zoo has never been so busy. Visitors pour in from all over the world to see them all together.

Nutz adapted to penguin life really quickly and enjoys diving in and out of the pool with Anton. Taddy visits Penguin Beach regularly, telling them all about the different things she encounters each day. She even brought Ray a small scarf and jumper so he'd always be warm!

Clyde and Diego love being penguins. But what they love even more than that is their family.

THE AUTHOR

Lawrence Prestidge is a popular children's author from Oxfordshire, best known for his children's novel *Terror at the Sweet Shop*. Educated at the University of Bedfordshire, Lawrence has previously worked with Disney as well as theatres across London. Lawrence visits many different Primary and Secondary schools throughout the year and travels all around the country doing so.

www.lawrenceprestidge.com
Twitter - LPrestidge7
Instagram - prestidgebooks
Facebook - Facebook.com/lawrenceprestidge